The Toronto Embryo

a novel

Judith Fournie Helms

Published by Snowy Day Publications

Hardy, Virginia

snowydaypublications@gmail.com

For my daughters, my granddaughters, and girls and
women everywhere, all of whom deserve better

Siempre adelante

Chapter 1

It may seem sacrilegious, but the truth is, I got pregnant on a church mission trip. It was in January of this year 2020, three years after the first Women's March on Washington and two months before I did something about it--this past weekend. At the beginning of the school year, I signed up through church to do service work at an orphanage in the Dominican Republic over winter break. When the time came, Mom had to stay home because she had a long trial starting right after the holidays, and Dad decided to stay with her. They both said they wanted to give me a little space to grow since I'm sixteen.

My best friend Claire planned to go with me but had to cancel at the last minute when her grandmother, a really cool lady, passed away. I said I'd go anyway. After all, it was a youth trip for kids my age from all over, so I was bound to meet someone I'd want to hang out with when we weren't working with the kids, cleaning toilets, painting buildings, or whatever they'd have us doing. Plus, I love to travel to new places. Ever since I was little, my favorite sound has been a suitcase zipper zipping. And, as Dad pointed out, it would look good on college applications. So, all-in-all, an easy decision.

My flight landed in the evening, and by the time I found my luggage on the carousel and got through customs, it was dark. We'd been told to carry as many suitcases as the airline would allow, and the contents were all supposed to be donations for the orphanage: clothes, crayons, markers, toys, books…really, anything. Apparently, nothing sent through the mail ever made it all the way, which really stinks. All we needed for ourselves were jeans, or shorts—knee length for modesty—and underwear. The program provided clean t-shirts for us each day. Cell phones weren't allowed, so I'd braced myself for an agonizing withdrawal.

An older woman from the orphanage met us and hustled us onto a rust-bucket bus for the two-hour ride. It was really stifling inside, but the windows were open, so once we got moving the fresh air blew in and saved us from suffocation. Because it was so dark, I saw just a little of the country on the bus trip. When we drove through towns, the harsh, pulsating florescent lights on the store signs jumped out at me, but, not knowing Spanish, I wasn't sure what they said. They seemed to be for restaurants and bars, and music and laughter gushed out of them.

Two family groups and I got to the complex after lights out, so it was basically pitch dark as we stepped off the bus. The woman led us around with an over-sized flashlight so we wouldn't walk into each other or a building. She told us to drop our large suitcases inside the door of a cinder block building, just inside the gates, which they used to store all the donations. I was handed a business card that said "!Gracias!" on one side and had the name and address of the orphanage on the other. All I had left was my backpack, which held just my clothes and personal items. I rummaged through it for my little pink pen-light, but the woman who pointed me to my bunkhouse told me I couldn't use it because I would wake up the other volunteers. So, I stumbled around pushing back mosquito netting and feeling the beds for an empty one. I must've accidentally felt up a dozen girls before I found a spot. Contrary to what I'd been promised, the mosquito net hadn't been hung, but lay in a pool on my bottom bunk. I felt all around the wooden bed frame and under the edges of the mattress above me, but I couldn't find a place to hang it up. I finally just wrapped it around my entire body, took a long breath of the sweet, humid night air and fell into a deep sleep.

I've never lived on a farm. But now I know the cock-a-doodle-doo at dawn thing is real, and somehow even more jarring than an alarm clock. Worse, you can't turn it off. When I opened my eyes, the bunkhouse was already filled with light. I lay on my back and scanned the space. There were no real walls--just screens attached to wooden rails, and a concrete floor. Maybe two dozen bunk beds with small suitcases and backpacks crammed between them. I quickly decided I liked the pioneer feel of it, but I was too spoiled to really enjoy it until I could wash my face and brush my teeth. One of the volunteers pointed me to the bathhouse and told me there'd only be cold water from the taps and in the shower. We weren't supposed to flush our toilet paper, but throw it in a trash can. And no flushing except for number two. That seemed pretty disgusting, but I certainly didn't want to be the one to screw up the plumbing. It was surprising to me how hard it was to break the habit of tossing the used toilet paper into the pot. Apparently, I wasn't the only one with this problem, since they'd placed a stick next to each toilet so we could fish out the soaking wet yellowish tissue and put it in the correct receptacle--gross. I was also told I had to go to a tank near the kitchen area to fill my water bottle. Then, and only then, could I brush my teeth. Nobody told me what would happen if I forgot and brushed with the tap water, but my imagination filled in the blanks.

There was no electricity in the bathhouse, so it was lit only by the sunshine that managed to squeeze through the foot or so of open space along the roofline. So even if anyone had brought makeup, there was no convenient place to put it on. The idea of a clean face being the only expectation felt darned good, and I knew my freckles added a little bit of color to my pale face. All the girls wore their hair in top-knots or pony-tails due to the heat and the fact that there was really no reason to fool with any other style.

Once I'd cleaned up and returned to the bunkhouse to make my bed, I caught a glimpse of tiny chrome hooks, hidden under the upper mattress, for my mosquito netting. I also found a neatly pressed, purple t-shirt under my pillow. So, fresh-faced, pony-tailed and outfitted in my official "VOLUNTEER" t-shirt, I went looking for breakfast. One of the male counselors saw me gawking around and came over to welcome me, walking stiffly as though his knees didn't bend properly. He said, "Purple. Perfect. You landed in the right bunk last night." It was funny because he spoke in a hushed voice, like he was giving me a top-secret mission. But his actual words just explained my work-unit assignment and when meals and breaks would be. I was supposed to find other purple t-shirts and ask them where our counselor had said to meet after breakfast.

I saw two boys seated at one of the picnic tables over plates of pancakes and a banana-like fruit I later learned was called a plantain. The boys had their backs to me, but one of them was definitely wearing a purple t-shirt. I saw no other purples around, so I took a really deep breath like I used to do before jumping off the high-dive, when moving forward was my only option. My heart was racing as I walked over, sat across from them and smiled. "Hi. My name's Eve. I was told to find a purple t-shirt and ask where I'm supposed to go after breakfast."

Both boys stood and then sat back down, which I thought was odd. Once they started speaking I understood why they were so polite. They weren't American. "Hello. I'm Gerhard, but Americans usually call me Jerry. It's nice to meet you, Eve." He turned toward his friend. "And this is Adam."

"Hi, Jerry. Adam, do you also have a special name for Americans to use?"

"Yes. Adam. It is very special." He laughed.

"Well, Adam, can you tell me what I'm supposed to do after breakfast?"

"Of course. My pleasure. But first, let me get for you a plate of breakfast. Yes?"

"Sure. Thanks."

Jerry stopped eating, waiting for Adam to return with my plate. After a minute of embarrassing silence, he said, "Adam and I are from Cologne, in Germany."

"I've never been there. Is it pretty?"

"Yes. Yes. Very beautiful. Where do you come from, Eve?"

"Oh, I'm from Chicago."

Adam had already returned since the serving table was only a few yards from us. He was handing my plate and glass of water to me. "Ah. Gangsters and guns."

I laughed. "Well, yeah. We do have too many guns. But Al Capone was a long time ago."

Adam just looked at me and said, "Of course." Then he laughed.

Both boys were very nice looking. Adam had the earnest face of a child and a gentle, reassuring smile. But the best thing was his laugh--hearty and unrestrained. He went on, "The purple t-shirts meet in twenty minutes, just under that tree." He pointed to a tall, solitary tree near the baseball field. "You hear a loud bell, so you know it is time."

"Great! Thanks." I started in on my pancakes but was really still trying to digest their looks. Adam was tall with light brown hair, clear blue eyes like the sky after a storm, and a slender build. Jerry was just a smidge shorter and heavier, with seaweed green eyes. I'd always been uncomfortable around good-looking guys, but somehow, those two weren't super-intimidating. Even so, it's just awkward meeting new people, so I worried about a silly thing. I thought I might get embarrassed when they both finished eating, and I was still chewing away. Luckily, they were thoughtful enough to keep sipping from their glasses of water, so I wouldn't be the only one with my mouth full.

"You know, Eve, I saw you arrive last night," said Adam.

"Really? How could you see anything in that blackout?"

"I will tell you a secret."

"Okay."

"I was sneaking back into my bunkhouse, which is just across from yours."

I couldn't imagine what he might have been up to in the pitch dark. "Sneaking back from what?"

Jerry added, "Yes. From what? I didn't know you snuck out."

"Well, this answer will probably disappoint you both. But I had just walked down the dirt road to an old mansion on the hill."

Jerry turned and pointed just beyond the orphanage entrance. "You mean that road, as opposed to all of the other dirt roads around here?"

"Yes. That one. The old house is closed up, and there is a fence and barbed wire around the...what is the word? Perimeter?" He smiled. "Anyway, I found a place I can get through."

"To do what?" I asked.

Adam looked around. No counselors were anywhere within earshot. He whispered anyway. "The house is on the side of a hill. I go to the top and lie down in the grass to look at the stars."

"Wait a minute," said Jerry. "You'd be devoured by the mosquitos—and I don't see a bite on you."

"Gerhard, give me a little credit. I take a mosquito net and just wrap myself in it. It works fine. No bite."

I said, "I can back Adam up on that, Jerry. The wrapping thing works."

"Wait. Were you there too?" Jerry squinted his eyes and cocked his head in exaggerated confusion.

"Of course not." I laughed. "I just had to use the wrap method last night since I got in after lights-out and couldn't see to hang my net." Since they said nothing, I went on, "So, how do you guys like it here?"

"The weather is sensational," said Jerry. "It hardly rains ever, and most of our days have been just like today—brilliant sun, clear sky." Both boys were already bronzed and had a healthy looking glow. Jerry saw me looking at their arms and added, "But we won't be showing off our tans back home." He pulled up his short sleeve to reveal the fair skin just beyond the edge. He laughed.

I said, "That's what we call a farmer's tan. If I get one, I'll definitely be hiding it once I get back to school and have to mingle with girls who went to Cancun--and probably didn't wear t-shirts when they sunbathed."

The boys laughed. Adam said, "The supply hut has lots of heavy-duty sunscreen. Your skin is very light, Eve. I don't want any of our group to have arms that match their purple t-shirts."

"I'll be careful. My mom sent me with SPF-50 and made it clear she expects me to use it. There are things I can hide from my parents, but they don't include my face and arms." There was a pause in the conversation that my nervousness pushed me to fill it in. "So, what do you think of the counselors?"

Adam said, "I mainly report to Jan, and she's great. Very organized. I mean, she keeps a lot of lists and charts. I don't actually see her interact with the boys all that much. I am not criticizing. Someone has to make sure the milk is delivered and the butcher is paid. And she has a friendly personality—efficient without being overbearing."

I turned and looked at Jerry. He said, "I mainly get my instructions from Thomas. He actually is a bit bossy, to say the truth. But, like Adam said, we can't all spend our days playing ball and taking the boys for ice cream. You will know Thomas because he walks very straight-legged, a bit like an automaton."

"I think I met him."

"But heck, he helps keep this place running, so I have no objection to work with him."

"Yes," said Adam. "I really don't care how the staff treats me, as long as they make it possible for me to really focus my energy on the kids." He looked at me and added, "I think you will be glad you came." I'd only gotten through breakfast on Day 1, and I was already glad I came. I just smiled and nodded.

We talked for a few more minutes. They both excused them-selves, and then cleared away my plate and utensils, as well as their own.

After breakfast, I returned to the bathhouse to wash my hands. Being a compulsive brusher, I also scrubbed my teeth again, careful to use the bottled water. I was surprised at how hard it was to resist putting my toothbrush under the faucet. I was fighting my muscle-memory and I realized how easy it would be to lose the battle—probably a very bad one to lose.

It was just a few minutes until I heard the bell, and I walked over to the tree Adam had pointed out. Five girls and three boys in matching purple t-shirts, all around my age, were milling around. I was disappointed Adam wasn't with them. As I stood there, waiting for something to happen, I appreciated that Adam and Jerry had been right about the weather. It re-minded me of Hawaii, when my parents and I had first stepped out of the airplane and a sweet, balmy, gardenia-scented blast of air welcomed us with a big hug. Of course, the orphanage grounds didn't remind me of the luxury resort grounds which were also part of our trips. But I felt a wave of happiness when it struck me that the little boys living in poverty in a third-world country enjoyed the same climate as rich Americans who travel to Pacific islands for it. Very cool.

A couple minutes passed and a twenty-something coun-selor arrived, clipboard in hand. She had very short blond hair and a very square jaw, and said her name was Jan. She wel-comed me and introduced all of us. The volunteers had been paired in such a way that each two-person team had at least one Spanish-speaker. Well, these turned out to be more like Spanish-studiers. I found out that one of the volunteer groups was a Spanish club from Cleveland. Jan told us we could speak Spanish with the boys as much as we wanted to, as long as we spent some time talking with them in English. Since the others had already been paired up, I was without a partner. Jan said, "Eve, please wait after we adjourn. Adam should be here soon. I asked him to help the little boys get ready for breakfast."

"So, Adam speaks Spanish?"

She nodded. "And, I think, at least three other languages."

"Really?"

"Actually, that's not unusual among our volunteers from Europe. He's been here for a month already, so he knows the drill."

"Oh. I thought the longest volunteer session was ten days."

"It is for regular volunteers. But we also have what we call 'long-term volunteers.' They can stay from one to twelve months."

"Wow. I must've missed that on your website. I guess I was focused on what would fit in during my winter break."

"Understandable. But, if you like it here, you could come back as a long-term during summer break or your summer before college. We also get some gap-year volunteers." She looked down at her clipboard and seemed to be itching to get back to whatever she was doing.

"Thanks. I'll keep that in mind." I walked around for a while looking for a good place to sit and wait for Adam. The breeze carried a delicate fragrance of flowers, probably from a neighbor's garden, since the grounds were limited to grass and dirt. Well, there were also palm trees mixed in with the leafy ones in front of the perimeter fence, but I had no idea if any of them gave off a floral scent. That was something I needed to look into. I decided to approach Jan again since she was still in the area, making notes on her pad. "Excuse me."

She looked up and smiled patiently. "Of course. How can I help you, Eve?"

"I was just wondering. How much longer will Adam be here?"

"He'll still be here when you leave. His commitment is through mid-August."

"Oh, great. Thanks." I couldn't believe my luck being assigned to work with a cute, overly polite guy. Maybe this trip was actually a brilliant idea. I had missed my parents while travelling, but now I was excited to be really on my own in an interesting Third World country. As poor as dirt, but with gorgeous weather and, I'd read, spectacular beaches. I looked forward to a beach day—a reward for the volunteers, which I'd been told we'd have later in the week

I sat down and leaned against the furrowed trunk of the towering tree to wait. After a few moments of mindlessly staring up at its leaves, I started really trying to identify it. Since I couldn't place it, I looked around for a leaf to study and found one on the ground, within reach. It was about seven inches long and had six opposite shiny leaflets with smooth edges. I still didn't recognize it, so I stuck it into the lower pocket of my cargo pants, hoping it would make it home intact so I could figure it out using my leaf identification book. That's when I laughed out loud and said, "Nerd." I was so relaxed, just sitting there. I'd never before felt such contentment just to be at the beginning of something. I had no idea that the something would threaten my future and my parents' marriage.

Chapter 2

That first morning, Adam gave me some background on the eight boys in our group, and then introduced me to them. Five-year-olds Carmelo and Domingo, were darling. They were the same height, but Carmelo was skinny and wiry, while Domingo looked like one of the chubby cherubs from those religious paintings by the masters. Javier and Vincent were both seven-year-olds, but Javier, who was from Haiti and had darker skin than the other boys, wouldn't make eye contact with me. Adam had told me he was teased for his complexion. He said the volunteers tried to discourage it, but it was really hard to fight the prejudice which had its roots deep in the culture. So, like in the United States.

Vincent was tall and slender, with glasses and a wrinkled forehead that made him look like he was deep in a thought. Adam had predicted I'd find him with his face in a book while the other boys played sports or goofed around. I was especially interested in working with Javier and Vincent. I figured both boys must get a lot of attention from the volunteers, especially the girls.

Adam had warned me that nine-year-old Pedro was a real clown, constantly goofing around, and that Jose, who was two years older, always egged the others on to see the hilarity. When they were introduced to me, Pedro made rabbit ears behind Jose's head, then elaborately bowed. Sure enough, Jose doubled over laughing.

Carmen, thirteen, and Alex, fifteen, remained a few yards from the group while the introductions were made. They stepped up to shake hands with me, smiled, and then immediately retreated from our little gathering. Maybe they were self-conscious since they both looked more like young men than the others. They just seemed kind of preoccupied. I'd learned the boys had to leave the orphanage at sixteen, and that Alex and Carmen were worried about being able to support themselves. I suppose I'd be preoccupied too if I were told I had to support myself—starting now. Alex was very handsome, athletic looking, and had killer dimples, and Carmen was also good looking, with light brown eyes and a lopsided smile. Each of the boys in our group spoke English pretty well, but—except for Vincent--needed a lot of help to read and write it.

On weekdays, Adam and I just had the two preschoolers in the mornings because the others were in public school until noon. So, I got to interact with Carmelo and Domingo that first morning while Adam was off at some meeting with the counselors and the long-terms. The boys and I sat down to make a list of activities they wanted to do, and they took turns checking each one off as we finished it. They chose to play board games, play "family," and have me read stories to them. They killed me at Memory. I actually wondered whether the little cards were marked somehow but didn't see any evidence of it. We were more evenly matched at Chutes and Ladders and Candy Land, both of which I'd loved as a child because they meant full attention from my parents. That memory made me a little sad—guilty, maybe—since I sat with two little guys who'd never get a mom's or dad's attention. While the constant parade of volunteers meant they'd always have someone to roll the dice and move the tiny markers with them, there was no way it was the same as having a parent to play with. I realized for the first time that I'd taken all of that family time for granted—not in the sense that I didn't appreciate it. More that I thought it was normal—what all children got.

The next activity, playing family, absolutely broke my heart. The game consisted of me playing the mom, and the boys playing my babies climbing on my lap to take a bottle, or my toddlers having an imaginary picnic with me, or my five-year-olds, going with me to the beach, the library, or the candy shop. I wasn't used to pure imagination games, but I got the hang of it pretty quickly and eventually became immersed in them. I was relieved that our remaining activity was for me to read books to them until lunch time.

Adam returned at 12:30 and the other six boys, having finished their school day, joined us. It was obvious they were all overjoyed to see him. Trying to pick up some tips on interacting with the older ones, I watched him intently all afternoon. He was very relaxed with them. Although he'd only been at the orphanage for a month, they looked up to him like he was their beloved older brother. Even Carmello and Domingo, who had claimed me as their pretend mom only hours before, were attracted to Adam like butterflies to the lavender in my mom's garden.

He coaxed outliers into the group, teased and joked, and was physical with the boys in ways that seemed really welcome. He threw the little ones up and caught them, rubbed the tops of the heads and high-fived the grammar school boys. He'd created a secret handshake for the older ones which was strictly between him and them. It went so fast and was so convoluted, I couldn't begin to untangle it. I know because I tried, alone in a bathroom stall, and had to laugh out loud at how ridiculous it looked.

We ran races, played basketball, and, at the end of the afternoon, made a circle in the grass where Adam led us in songs I didn't know. After dinner, we played a baseball game against another volunteer's group. Vincent sat with me on the bleachers where I cheered our team, and he read a child's version of *Gulliver's Travels*. At the start of the seventh inning, Adam threw me his glove and told me to take left field. He became the cheering section, and I prayed the ball wouldn't come to me. I'm sure the boys were disappointed at the substitution, but they didn't let it show. Adam probably felt safe making the switch since our team was ahead by seven runs. I know how to play ball, and I'm not terrible at it. It's just one of the sports I prefer not to do in public. My prayer was answered, and I was also walked when I got up to bat. So no disaster occurred and the boys were thrilled with their victory over their friends. I wanted to understand how Adam made everything he did with the boys seem so easy.

Walking back to our bunkhouses that evening, I asked him why he connected so well. He smiled and said, "I have four younger brothers."

"You're the oldest?"

"Yes. I turned eighteen in October and my youngest brother is five. So, a wide range."

"Wow. How do your parents do it?"

"Do what?"

"I don't know. How do they keep everything orderly with five boys?"

Adam stopped for a moment and looked at me. I couldn't help noticing his eyes were the exact same shade as the sky. He said, "You, I think, have not lived with little boys."

"You're right. I'm an only child."

"I see. Well, it is not orderly. More like controlled chaos."

"Does your mom stay home with the little ones, or work outside the home?" I hoped he wouldn't be annoyed that I was prying.

"Mother is a teacher of mathematics for what you call middle school. Father too. Well, he teaches science at the same school. So, they have more time at home than some other professions, like doctor or lawyer."

"My dad's a doctor and my mom's a lawyer. And you're right. They both have pretty long hours. And they always have their laptops open at home." I sighed. "When I was little I had a nanny."

"Not a relative?"

"No. We don't live near any of our relatives. My parents dropped me off at Martha's house. She had two daughters near my age. It was good. They were like my sisters when I was younger. It was fine. Why? Who took care of you when your parents were working?"

"Grandmother and grandfather. She was always spoiling us and he only pretended to be strict. I have no complaints."

We'd arrived at the bunkhouses, but I delayed saying good night. "Well, Adam, you may not realize it, but you have a real gift with children. You're really amazing with them."

"I don't believe I am unusual. Think about it, Eve. Who would come to work at an orphanage if he or she didn't have a desire to be with children?"

I just smiled and nodded, thinking my reasons for coming weren't nearly as altruistic as his. The truth was that I came more for me, and he came more for them. That was a big difference, and I hoped his commitment to service would rub off on me. We both said, "Good night," and walked toward our separate screen doors.

I wasn't pathetic with the kids. They were all adorable. I played catch with them, read to them in English, and helped the little ones tie their shoes. And we spent hours drawing and coloring. At least I was pretty good at drawing, so I could sketch things that were fairly identifiable, and then the boys would try to give me the English words. I'd chosen Latin in school, but I couldn't use my lack of Spanish skills as an excuse for being a little awkward with the boys, since they could speak to me in English. It was more that little boys were new to me and I just didn't click with them like Adam did. They were respectful, but seemed shy around me, probably reflecting my nervousness back on me. I really wanted to get it right, and I hoped I could learn how to from him. He wasn't like any boy I'd ever known. He didn't just make the boys happy, he made me happy.

Chapter 3

On my third day, Adam asked if I was interested in sneaking out with him to stargaze from his spot on the hill. I was thrilled, both at the idea of doing something out of character like sneaking out, and because I loved doing anything with him.

I knew I'd never make it past twenty-four bunk beds and out the squeaky screen door of the bunkhouse without being seen. If I acted like I was on my way to the toilet, someone might be awake and notice I hadn't come back. My plan was to hide in the bathhouse and never go in for bed. So, I'd pulled the cliché trick from the movies and stuffed my pillow and some extra towels into an Eve-shape under my blanket. The mosquito netting encasing my bunk really helped, since you could barely see through it. I'd found some extra nets in the storage building and had wrapped one around my mid-section under my t-shirt. Then I'd sprayed myself with repellant for the walk. It helped tremendously that I'd made no real friends other than Adam. Everyone was pleasant enough, but the others had all come with groups or at least a buddy. Now I saw that my social awkwardness had been to my advantage. Nobody was looking for me.

We'd agreed to wait for fifteen minutes after the recorded bugle sounded for "lights out" and then make our way, separately, to the side gate with the rusted lock that wouldn't close. I hugged the perimeter and darted from one tree to another, the way I imagined an army ranger would do it. There was usually a guard about a quarter mile away at the front gate, but Adam said the guy was often away from his post tending to some little emergency or other. Once we'd both arrived at the side gate, we scanned the grounds for any movement. We had a clear line of sight all the way to the front of the complex, and the guard wasn't in view. Comfortable he wouldn't hear the squeak of the gate opening and closing, we slipped out.

It was a warm, clear night. There was just enough light for us to follow the dirt road without needing to use a flashlight. Nothing but fields on both sides of us. I just followed him, not sure what was going to happen. After walking for about twenty minutes, Adam pointed to a path that branched off from the road. He said, "It's just here."

We entered an area of brush and small trees. The trail took us up several hundred yards and then switched back, continuing at a sharper angle. As we rounded a large clump of bushes, we had to step through an opening in the barbed wire fence. It was only about eighteen inches square, so we had to move really slowly to avoid getting stuck. I caught a glimpse of the old mansion to our left. Lit by moonlight, it looked huge—about the size of my high school, and it had large white columns. It was obvious the house didn't remotely blend with its surroundings.

"Have you explored it?"

"No. And I don't really plan to, Eve. I have no interest to disturb anyone's property. My only goal is to get to the highest spot around to enjoy the stars." He smiled, and his teeth and the whites of his eyes glowed before he turned away. We finished the hike single file trying to avoid the sticker bushes, finally arriving at a small clearing at the top. As best I could make out, it was mainly grass and weeds, and a few pieces of wood scattered about.

Adam reached in the small backpack he'd carried and

pulled out a dark sheet. He whipped it until it fell flat and then motioned for me to sit. He said, "The best way to do this is to lie on your back." Something about his phrasing made me feel apprehensive for the first time since I'd met him. After all, I'd only known him for a few days. I lay back until I was resting on my elbows, hoping Adam was really who I thought he was.

"Did you bring the thing?"

I'm embarrassed to say my mind raced to "condom." There was no good reason for this since Adam hadn't even tried to hold my hand. And I had never brought a condom anywhere in my life.

"What thing?"

"Your mosquito net."

A little hiccup of a laugh escaped, which I hoped he hadn't noticed. "Oh, yeah. I have it wound around my middle, like an inner tube. By the way, thanks for not commenting on my sudden weight gain."

He laughed. "Here, stand up and let me help you. You have to make sure you're completely covered, but not tight." Somehow, he got me fully mummified without actually touching me. After I sat back down, Adam wrapped himself and then joined me, lying back maybe a foot away from me. He must've landed the sheet on a patch of grass, because there were no rocks or twigs sticking into me. We arranged ourselves so only our eyes were uncovered, like the Muslim women in the middle-East. He lay there searching the night sky for a few moments before speaking again. "Eve, do you know the constellations?"

"I'm pretty good at the Big and Little Dippers. Oh, and the North Star. But that's about the extent of it."

"Great! Can you find them for me?"

I searched the sky for the brightest star I could find, hoping it was the North Star. Then I visually arranged the rest of the Little Dipper until I was satisfied I probably wouldn't embarrass myself. I pointed and said, "There's the Little Dipper. The North Star's at the end of its handle."

"Yes." He paused and added, "Did you know the North Star is named Polaris and is relied on for navigation?"

"No. Why?"

"Because it actually is the northernmost star in the sky. But the crazy thing is that Polaris wasn't always the North Star, and it will be usurped by Vega in 12,000 years."

"Well, that's a long time to hold onto the title. I imagine it'll be hard to give up."

"True. But 14,000 years after that, Polaris takes it back."

"You're kidding. We're talking about something that won't happen for 26,000 years?"

"Yes. Why not?"

"It just seems somehow both fascinating and irrelevant."

"What do you mean?"

"Well, can you see humans surviving for 26,000 years without either blowing ourselves up or letting global warming destroy the planet?"

"No. I really can't imagine that. Sadly. Since usually I am an optimist."

"Exactly."

"But, Eve, that doesn't make it irrelevant. Polaris will still be there, even if we humans are long gone."

"I know. But, isn't it like the tree falling in the forest?"

"I see. You're suggesting the importance of what happens

in the universe is based on our knowing about it?"

"I never really thought about it. But before we had telescopes, lots of stars we didn't know about still existed," I said.

"Yes," replied Adam.

"But their existence just didn't matter to humans—since we knew nothing about them. I mean, reality is still reality, but if it's unknown, it can't be of interest to humans. Sort of, by definition."

"Of course, there is much that is unknown in the universe right now. Or, it will happen after we are no longer around. But, it isn't our knowledge of what will happen in 26,000 years that makes it real."

"But Adam, our knowledge is what makes it real to us—to people."

"So, you believe what we focus on is real to us, and what we don't focus on is not?"

We had both been staring at the sky. I turned toward Adam and said, "Exactly." I laughed. "I do see your point. The universe is real before, during, and after the brief time humanity hangs out in the picture. Of course, you're right. I'm just saying we humans are very human-centric. So, I can't imagine there'd be much popular interest in what'll happen in 26,000 years. It's just not how we think. Seriously, there are plenty of people who still deny global warming—and it's already here."

"That's true. But it doesn't make the narrow view right."

"Not especially right. But especially human." I appreciated how good it felt to be able to share my thoughts with Adam, without embarrassment. I'd already stopped second-guessing whether I was being stupid. Talking with him was almost as comfortable as gabbing with Claire. Anyway, I felt we'd pretty much exhausted the point. "So, what other star facts do you know?"

"Too many. It has been a hobby of mine since I was little."

"How little?"

"Seven or eight, probably."

"That's very cool. So, tell me something interesting."

He laughed. "Remember, you asked for it. But you must tell me when it is too much."

"Oh, don't worry. I will."

"First of all, the common use of the word 'constellation' is a little off. Actually, the Big Dipper and the Little Dipper are examples of asterisms. You see, an asterism is just a pattern of stars with a popular name. The asterisms fall within the perimeter of a constellation. The sky has 88 constellations. They are based on the asterisms of Greek and Roman mythology."

"An example, please."

"Yes. The constellation you know as Cancer is really the asterism Cancer, plus a region around it containing millions of stars."

"I had no idea. That's really interesting. But, I actually love the word constellation. Would your inner-astrologer be offended if we just call the patterns constellations?"

"No. Not at all. Most people wouldn't know 'asterism,' So, we should definitely go with the word you love. What we call Big Dipper is only the larger part of what we call Big Bear. The same with Little Dipper."

I sighed, feeling a special kind of solace I've only experienced looking at the heavens. And I realized I hadn't done it nearly enough. I also knew I needed to keep the conversation going since I wasn't quite ready for whatever might happen if we quit talking. "Let me guess…Little Bear."

"Exactly. Now look up at the Big Dipper."

I took a moment to find it again. "Got it."

"Do you see the two bright stars to the right of it?"

"Yeah."

"Look carefully. The two bright stars at the end of the Big Dipper make a line, pointing at the North Star."

"I never noticed that before."

"It's just an easy way to find it." Adam paused. "Are you sure you want me to keep talking about this?"

"Of course. Why wouldn't I?"

"I don't want you to think I am showing myself off."

"Well, you already did that with the asterism thing." I laughed. "Anyway, I'm loving getting to know the stars a little better." I thought, *and you.*

"Okay then. I will tell you the myth of Little and Big Bears."

"Great."

"Yes. Well, the Big and Little Bears are actually called Ursa Major and Ursa Minor."

"Makes sense. Since ursa means bear in Latin."

"Right. There is not only one myth, but I will tell you my favorite."

As Adam was talking, I kept my eyes on the stars, and drank in every word he said. But I was also noticing other things: a slight dampness in the breeze, which I imagined having been carried to me all the way from the ocean, and the gauzy texture of the mosquito net which made me think of how a bride's veil might feel. It was like I was hyper-aware, or maybe I was just hyper-alive.

"Ursa Minor is Arcus, the son of Zeus and the maiden, Callisto, to whom Zeus was not married. When Arcus was fifteen, he was hunting in the forest and came across a strange looking bear which was looking him right in the eye. So he prepared to shoot it. But another god, who knew it was actually Callisto, who had been turned into a bear after Arcus' birth, stepped in to stop him. Arcus was then also turned into a bear, and he and his mother were both taken up to the sky."

"Wow."

"There's more. Juno became jealous those two were given such a great honor and took his revenge by getting Poseidon to agree to forbid both bears from ever bathing in the sea. This is why, through all time, Big Bear and Little Bear never dip beneath the horizon when seen from the north latitude."

"But wait. Why had Callisto been turned into a bear in the first place?"

"A myth has it that Zeus's jealous wife, Hera, was the reason. It may be that Callisto was transformed into a bear by Zeus to protect her from his wife. But, it is more likely that Zeus wanted Callisto gone to avoid detection by his wife. That part is unclear to me."

"How could you know, for sure?" I was still thinking about Arcus and his mom. "So, being thrust into the sky is an honor?"

"Yes. Definitely."

"Well, that makes sense. Immortality, beauty, and getting admired...for as long as there will be humans."

"Wait. You are circling back to our last argument?"

I pretended to be huffy. "Certainly not. Anyway, I don't

believe in arguments. Only discussions."

"You are able to live your life that way, Eve?"

"So far. I mean, I like passion in discussions. But I just think conversation should always be respectful. Yelling's always seemed counterproductive to me. I guess I'm more into the power of reason and analysis. Maybe that's why I love science so much."

"Really? I do too." A few moments of silence passed and he added, "Then, do your parents argue or discuss?"

"Oh, they're big discussers. Honestly, I know of only one real argument. It was three years ago. Basically, about politics."

"Ah. So they have different political views?"

"Actually, they do. See, Dad's a Republican and Mom's a Democrat. But that's not what they were arguing about. It's just that they're both feminists to the core."

"So they weren't arguing about that either."

"Not per se. It was about abortion. My mom's a pro-life feminist."

"Hm."

"I know. A lot of people don't even believe there is such a thing."

"And your father is pro-abortion?"

"They call it 'pro-choice.' But, yes. Well, my folks usually leave each other alone about it. But three years ago, we all wanted to fly to DC for the Women's March on Washington."

"I remember. Wasn't that just after President Trump was elected?"

"Exactly. But when Mom learned her pro-life sign wouldn't be welcome, she decided not to go with us."

"She didn't think she could go and support her other

feximist issues?"

I smiled to myself. "That was one of my dad's arguments. See, the discussion started at the dinner table. But after I'd gone up to my room, they took it into the family room, and it turned into an argument."

"Then how do you know what they said, if you weren't there?"

I hoped Adam wouldn't think I was a creep for what I was going to tell him. "The truth is, there's an air vent between the floors and I can actually hear everything from the family room. Maybe I should've told them, but I was too embarrassed to admit I knew they were arguing. The thing is, it had never happened before. And they were into it before I could stop and think through what to do."

"Hm."

I wasn't sure what Adam's response meant, but I decided to go ahead and finish the story. "So, Mom said she was upset with the Movement for excluding half the women in the country over an issue that their consciences couldn't let them ignore. See, I knew the abortion thing was really important to her. I just didn't know it was more important than going on a family trip. Dad really wanted her to come with us, but she dug in her heels. She wanted me to have the experience of the march though, so she said we should go ahead without her."

"What happened?"

"Dad and I went. I made a boring sign in bubble letters, 'women's rights = human rights.' It turned out that Dad had been right about one of his arguments. It did feel empowering to me. When my dad and I got to the top of the escalator at the Smithsonian stop, I could see crowds in every direction.

The station we'd planned to get off at was so packed that no one else could even get off the trains, since we were blocked by a wall of people. There were homemade signs everywhere. Mine was probably the least interesting, but I was so glad I'd brought one. It was nearly impossible to walk, but we inched our way to a spot in front of one of the teletrons to see what was happening on the main stage."

"It sounds very exciting."

"Definitely. We were in the middle of a sea of people who all cared about women. Then everyone spontaneously combusted into songs and chants. THE coolest thing I've ever seen. Honestly, it felt exactly like all of us together were flexing a giant muscle."

"It must have been beautiful."

"It really was. I'm so glad I got to go."

"Did your father still feel like your mother should've gone?"

"No. He said she'd been right not to come with us. All of the abortion rights signs would've infuriated her. Realistically, there was no way she could've just focused on the other issues."

"Did you ever tell them you could hear them the night they argued?"

"Actually, it never came up again. I mean, they never had another argument, so it seemed silly to embarrass them—and myself-- for no reason. Anyway, do your parents argue, Adam?"

"Only about one subject. But, yes, we can hear them in our bedrooms."

"Politics?"

"No. Never. It is always about money... the lack of it.

Probably three or four flare-ups a year. But, I can't hear it clearly enough to know exactly what they're saying. We get just enough to know that the gist is that we don't have enough money."

"I'm sorry you and your brothers have to hear that."

"Yeah. Me too."

"So, how does that make you feel about arguments?"

"That I prefer discussions. And at a volume that can't be heard by the children."

It hit me that Adam must've paid his own way to the orphanage. "So, did you have to pay for your flight to come here from Germany?"

"I did fund-raising."

"Like car-washes and bake-sales?"

"No. More like talking to people from our church about what I wanted to do, and asking for contributions."

"That must've been hard. I mean, it's way more efficient, but what did you think about it?"

"That I would prefer to be able to pay my own way."

He said nothing further, and I felt bad for having brought it up. So, I asked him to tell me about another constellation.

"Sure. Use the Big Dipper as a guide. Follow the curve of its handle down to the southeast until you come to a very bright star."

"I see it."

"Okay. Good. The star is called Arcturus. Now, continue the arc to the next bright star, Spica. I like to remember by the phrase I read: 'Follow the arc to Arcturus, then speed on to Spica.' Well, Spica is one of the stars of the asterism, Virgo, which is Latin for virgin."

"Right. I just never connected the Latin word with the constellation. Tell me about Virgo."

"Many of the stars of Virgo are very dim, but Spica is bright and blue-white, so it's helpful for finding the constellation. Virgo is seen as having angel-like wings, with an ear of wheat in her left hand. And Virgo is just next to Libra—we will get to her."

"Oh good. I'm a Libra."

"Really? What is your birthday?"

"October 20th. What's yours?"

"October 7th."

"Hm. So, does Virgo have a myth?"

"More than one. I prefer the Greek one, which associates her with the Greek virgin goddess of justice, the daughter of Zeus. She lived in the Golden Age. She was born mortal, and assigned to rule over human justice. Everything was wonderful. Peace and prosperity. Humans were never to grow old."

"There would be pros and cons to that."

"Agreed. Anyway, Zeus overthrew his father and that started the Silver Age."

"Not so prosperous and peaceful?"

"Correct. Zeus started the four seasons."

"Good for him. I love the changing of the seasons."

"So do I. Of course, not as good for the crops. But the real problem was that humans no longer honored the gods as they had before. Virgo grew more and more concerned, and finally gave a major speech to all humans. She warned them of the problems to come if they abandoned the ideals of their parents and grandparents. Eventually she got disgusted with people and flew to the mountains, turning her back on them.

The Bronze and Iron Ages came next and humans started having wars against each other. That was the last straw. She flew to the heavens, where we can still see her at night."

"I like Virgo, the virgin. She saw what was coming and warned everyone," I said.

"But then she flew away to the mountains."

"Yes. But maybe the big warning was the best she could do. I just think you get to a point where people have to want to follow good advice. Without that, you might as well quit talking and fly to the mountains."

"You are speaking from experience?"

"It's just that my best friend's father is an alcoholic. It's been so many years that Claire and her mom have tried to help him—to reason with him, give him ideas, incentives, support. It just won't work. I don't think anything can work for him until he wants to change."

"That's so sad."

"Yeah. I've come to believe that most things are like that. Help's great once we're ready for it, Adam."

"I've seen it too. Even once the person makes the decision to change, it is very hard. But, without the decision, it is impossible."

I thought to myself for a moment. "Well, maybe we agree so much because we're both Libras. What do you think of astrology?"

"I always think of it as being like fortune cookies."

"The fortune part, not the cookie part, right?"

"Yes, I totally believe in the cookie part. But the fortune part is just there for us to play with. And the qualities that are supposedly set by the stars, and the kinds of connections between people with different signs—it is all there for us to have fun with. So, we subconsciously select whatever seems true to focus on, and ignore, or rationalize away anything we don't like. It can be entertaining. But I would never base a decision on it. Do you follow it?"

"I don't really understand enough about it to believe in it or not. I just know I'm a Libra and my precious birthstone is opal. Actually, I'm not sure exactly what a precious stone is. It's just something I read. So, what do you know about Libra? I mean the constellation, not my sign."

He laughed. "Not that much. We can see Libra just next to the hand of Virgo. Remember, Virgo was the goddess of justice, and had scales as the emblem of her office. So, Libra is basically the representation of balance and justice. Just old-fashioned scales. I think that is all I can offer on Libra—the constellation."

"No. That's great. It fits perfectly with Virgo. I like it."

He turned over onto his side, facing me, and pulled the netting away from his face. He said, "Eve, I have really enjoyed that you've been interested in my hobby. Or you have been kind and pretended to be." He laughed. "But we really must use some of our time up here...."

I had no idea where he was headed, or even where I wanted him to be headed.

"It's just that it is very nice to lie here and gaze at the stars in silence. Is this okay with you?"

"Oh my gosh, yes. I would love to do that." Now it was clear that Adam wasn't going to make any moves, I really did relax. At first, I half-feared I'd be so distracted by the beautiful boy lying beside me that I wouldn't be able to fully absorb the stargazing experience. But I soon lost my awareness of anything but the heavens. I don't know how long we lay, searching the layers of brightness which stretched into infinity, since I really felt like I'd been transported into another dimension.

I startled when he whispered, "It is time to head back."

"Oh sure. I was just feeling like I'd joined the bears and Virgo and all the rest up there. I've never felt anything quite like this."

"Yes. It is magical up here and always hard for me to leave." He helped me up, the first time our hands had touched. I really hadn't expected the current that shot through me. I think I managed to cover it up. I hoped. We both unwrapped ourselves from the netting. He shook out and folded the sheet and stuffed it and his net back into his backpack. I re-tied mine around my waist, thinking it was still the best way to hide it in case anyone would happen to see me. We walked down in comfortable silence. At least, it was comfortable for me. I felt as light as a balloon, relaxed and safe--happy.

Once we reached the gate, I said, "Thanks so much for taking me, Adam. It was magical." I smiled and he opened the gate just enough for us to slip through.

"It was my pleasure. Good night, Eve." There was a long pause, and just as I was about to take off for the tree cover, he added, "Tomorrow?"

I stopped and turned toward him. "Definitely!" I was so thrilled he invited me again that I had trouble not skipping back to my bunkhouse. Being heard sneaking back in didn't worry me. I could always claim I'd just gone to the bathroom, and whoever saw my return must've missed my tiptoeing out, minutes before. "Sorry for waking you...blah, blah, blah." No one said a word and I fell asleep thinking of Adam.

Chapter 4

I didn't see him again until after breakfast. That day we worked together, as usual, but we were surrounded by other volunteers most of the day. Later that afternoon, Adam and I rounded up some of the boys who especially loved baseball for some practice. Outfielders threw the ball around, and a pitcher tried his stuff out on our strongest batter, Alex. It was a bad plan.

Maybe twenty minutes into practice, I was at short stop, throwing the ball around the bases with some of the boys. I could see Adam in the outfield, coaching the fielders practicing their long throws. Carmen was at center field watching a ball being thrown to him from right field. At the same time, Alex hit a powerful low fly ball, which Carmen didn't see coming. Suddenly, I saw Adam dive at Carmen so they both ended up on the ground. The ball caught Adam just behind his right shoulder as he flew through the air. It sure looked like it would've hit Carmen in the head, if Adam hadn't used his body to intercept it. I ran up to ask both of them if they were okay.

Carmen was surprised, but not hurt. He laughed and said, "If Adam hadn't knocked me down, I'd be great!"

Adam said, "No injury to report," and smiled at me.

I think he didn't want Alex to feel bad. But the truth is, he'd probably saved Carmen from serious injury--or worse. I could tell from the way he moved that Adam's bruise hurt, but he never mentioned it. I couldn't help myself. I was mentally tallying his virtues.

Once the lights-out bugle was played, I snuck out, just like the night before. The coast was clear, so we followed the same path: down the dirt road, up the trail, through the gap in the barbed wire and on to our spot. My heart was racing the whole time, since I knew we were headed for heaven. I realized it was because of Adam, rather than the actual heaven we were about to stare into, but the combination was pretty wonderful. We had gorgeous, clear weather again, and the night sounds surrounded us. Crickets and tree-frogs chattered away like tiny raindrops on a tin roof. Hoot owls echoed in the distance and there was a random rustling in the bushes and trees that made me glad I wasn't alone. I smelled the soil in the air, though I didn't know how the island stayed so lush when it never seemed to rain.

When we got to our spot, Adam pulled a dark blanket out of his backpack, along with his net.

"You've upgraded!"

He laughed as he whipped it until it lay flat. "I thought this would be more comfortable for you."

"The sheet was really fine. But thanks, Adam."

We both wrapped ourselves in our nets and got into position to stargaze. My heart was still racing, and I was thrilled we were covered by darkness so Adam wouldn't see my blushed neck. He lay down closer than the night before, only inches from me. I could feel the blanket tighten under me as he spread out on his back, which somehow embarrassed me. So, I quickly blurted out. "What's another one with a great myth behind it?"

Adam pulled his right arm out of his cocoon and I startled a little, which I hoped he hadn't noticed. I knew I had to calm myself down so I'd seem like a normal person, rather than a school-girl with a crush (which I was). He pointed at a spot in the sky. "Lyra. It is fairly easy to pick out because it has the very bright star, Vega, in it, and is the shape of the musical instrument, the lyre." I could see Vega, but couldn't really make out the lyre. "The instrument was owned by Apollo's son, Orpheus. A very sad story though."

I consciously slowed my breathing. "That's okay. I love the stories."

"All right. So, Orpheus played the lyre so beautifully that everyone was charmed by the music he made. He fell deeply in love with a young woman and they were married. But, while she was wandering through the woods one day, she was chased by a man and ended up getting bitten by a snake. She died of it. Orpheus was so devastated that he found a way to contact the king and queen of the Underworld."

"I didn't realize the Underworld had a king and queen."

"Oh yes. A regular kingdom down there." Adam spoke with mock seriousness, as though he'd popped by recently. "Orpheus begged them to let him take his wife back to the land of the living. They were so impressed with his music that they agreed, but only if he would promise not to look at her until the two of them reached the earth's surface. But, as he led her by the hand, he could tell she was still limping from the snake wound. He was so worried for her that, just as they were arriving, he turned back to look. She slipped back into the Underworld. He was so heartbroken that he rejected all women in favor of little boys."

"Yuck."

"Yes. And very bad for Orpheus. The women became so angry they killed him and threw his head, and his lyre, into the sea. But love won out since he was sent to the Underworld where he got to spend eternity with his wife. And Jupiter took the lyre from the sea and cast it into the sky."

"That's not really so sad. They were together in the end."

"I guess you're right. But with very sad parts."

"Like real life then." I searched the sky for another bright star which might be important in a constellation. I slipped my arm out of its enclosure and pointed, realizing there were now two uncocooned arms on the loose. "What's that one, Adam?"

"I think you are pointing at the only constellation which is broken into two pieces. It is Serpens Cauda and Serpens Caput. Serpens is, of course, serpent."

"Caput is head, and Cauda is tail. Right?"

"Yes. The head is the part to the west, and it has that bright star in it. The tail is to the east. The giant snake is being held by Asclepius. The myth is that he killed a snake. He then saw another snake place an herb on the dead one and bring it back to life."

"Impressive."

"Yes. Asclepius was so inspired by it that he used the same technique to bring people back to life. After that, his healing powers could raise the dead pretty reliably. So, since ancient times, the image of a snake entwined on a staff has been the symbol for medicine."

"I've seen that. But I didn't know where it came from."

"It is a universal sign."

"Well, that's a great story. And I love the thought of saving lives. It's something I'd like to be a part of someday."

"That's interesting. I feel that too, Eve."

"Are you saying you want to be a doctor?"

"I do, actually. Science interests me. Like the stars, it is fun to know about it. But doing hands-on medicine is how I hope to spend my life."

I turned my head toward him. "I love science at the cellular level. I guess it's more comfortable for me to work with a microscope than an actual person. Why do you think you want to be hands-on?"

He took a moment, and then sighed. "I have an aunt who has rheumatoid arthritis and lupus. Truly, Eve, she is in constant pain. She weighs probably forty kilos…about ninety pounds. She's had four back surgeries because her spine is basically disintegrating and they're trying to keep it together with plates and screws, and even cement. Her hands are contracted."

"What's that?"

"I would describe it that they are frozen in claw positions. Her lower legs swell and liquid comes out of the skin. It is called 'weeping edema.'"

"That's terrible. I'm so sorry, Adam."

"That's not all. She also has chronic heart failure and her heart is so weak that she wears a pace-maker and a defibrillator implanted below her skin just under her collar bone. As you may imagine, it's not exactly hidden there."

"How old is she?"

He took a moment before answering. "Aunt Bertha is fifty-five years."

"She's my parents' age."

"And close to my parents'. But the remarkable thing is, she never complains. In fact, she says she is the luckiest person…to have her husband and my two cousins. To be able to do the reading she loves so much. She told me she reads a book almost every day."

"She's incredible, Adam. I wish I knew her."

"Knowing her has changed me. Now that I'm old enough

to understand what is happening with her, I can't go back to not knowing. I want to fight for her, Eve. I want to fight for the people like her--people whose bodies betray them."

I thought about that. "Then she's given you a gift. You know what you want to do, and it's become a passion for you. Most of the kids I know have no idea what they want to do."

"You are not clear about your work with cells?"

"I'm pretty clear. But I don't think I'll feel passion for it until I have a specific mission. But, if I had one that was important to me, I think I'd want to fight for it too."

We agreed to take the rest of our time to focus quietly on the stars. But first I had to quiet my mind, which insisted on reviewing Adam's virtues. My chest felt swollen, as though my heart would explode with how much I cared for the beautiful, kindhearted boy lying beside me. I searched for constellations to concentrate on, and eventually my heart-rate slowed and I was free to float upward.

By the time we made it back to the orphanage grounds and I slid into my lower bunk, I was wiped out from a combination of the excitement of being with Adam, and my greedy hunger for more.

Chapter 5

The next day at lunch, Adam asked me if I'd be willing to skip the volunteers' beach outing the following day to stay and help him with a group of the boys. Of course, we couldn't all just go off to the beach and leave the orphans to fend for themselves. I'd really been looking forward to seeing one of the promised "stunning white-sand beaches with clear, turquoise-tinted water," and I wished some other long-term would stay back so Adam and I could go to the beach together. But since that wasn't an option, I chose more time with Adam, especially since there wouldn't be tons of other volunteers around us every minute.

"You are sure you're willing to give up your beach day, Eve?"

"Absolutely. I've seen tons of beaches. But spending time with these boys is once in a lifetime." I had no idea if Adam realized I was actually referring to one boy in particular. I supposed there was no reason he should have.

"Good," said Adam. "The beach-goers leave after breakfast tomorrow and will be gone until dinner time. We'll have sixteen boys in our group. The other groups of sixteen are going into town, so our group will be the only one here on the grounds. I have ideas for some special activities."

The next morning, I couldn't wait for the buses to leave for the beach. I didn't see Adam at breakfast and assumed he was getting things ready. When the activities bell rang, I spotted him under the tall tree, holding a clipboard. Boys ran toward him from all over, knowing the day would be different from the rest. I walked up to him, saluted, and said, "Ready for orders."

He smiled and handed me the clipboard. "Hi, Eve. Could you please make sure everyone is here? I will be right back."

Since I didn't really know the extra eight boys, I explained that I wanted them to yell, 'Si!' when I called their names. I was just finishing when Adam returned with a large canvas bag filled with jump ropes. Finally--an activity I was good at. We all walked over to the weathered blacktop basketball court to jump. There was no shade in the area, so I pulled my sunglasses out of my cargo pants pocket. The boys didn't even squint and I wondered if their eyes had just gotten used to the intense sunlight. I questioned whether that was even possible and vowed to google it once I got home.

The older boys took to it right away. When I saw how hard it was for the little guys to synchronize their arm motions with the jumping, I asked Alex to help me turn a long rope for them. We started by swinging it back and forth slowly until they got the hang of it. Then I had Javier help Alex turn it while I demonstrated for the little guys. I heard Pedro say something, and suddenly the rope was speeding up until, finally, I couldn't jump fast enough. The boys were all laughing their heads off. I grabbed Pedro's hands and said, "Vamanos," hoping it meant what I thought it did. I pulled him in to jump double-dutch with me, and then the rope was being turned really slowly. That worked fine for him, but was actually even harder for me than the racing rope. I leaped out and nudged Jose in to jump with Pedro. They were both laughing and jumping, and the boys all clapped the rhythm for them.

Once everyone had caught on, we went on to relay jump races, cat and mouse, and helicopter. Their favorite was action jumping where the jumper had to do an action, while jumping. Jumping with eyes closed and taking off their sneakers got the most shrieks, but trying to burp while jumping was a close third. I looked up to see Adam taking pictures of the boys, and of me. He'd been assigned to use the director's camera to take pictures of the orphans from time to time to try to get some charming shots for publicity. I had trouble imagining any photo of those beautiful children not being charming.

It was clear to me the volunteer who'd brought the jump ropes had been brilliant. Once we were all worn out from the cardio workout, Adam did something unusual. Rather than having all the ropes returned to the canvas bag he'd brought them in, he made sure everybody had one. We all walked over to the covered picnic table area and Adam had each of them write his name in black marker on one of the wooden handles of his rope.

Adam had told me that each boy kept everything he owned in his own small cubbyhole. Literally, everything he owned. And by "small" I mean about fifteen inches square. We volunteers were not allowed to give the boys any gifts. But, somehow, Adam had convinced the director to let the boys keep the jump ropes. I guess she must've realized that for a boy to get out a jump rope when he needs to burn off steam beats most alternatives.

Once all of the boys had returned from depositing their jump ropes in their cubbies, Adam announced a lemonade and pretzel break. The boys descended on the wooden picnic tables and began lying or sitting with legs dangling, picking at each other the way boys do. While everyone was snacking, Adam announced a game of truth or dare. It was similar to the game we have at home. Someone would be on the spot. He would have to honestly answer all of the questions thrown at him. If he refused to answer, or seemed not to be telling the truth, the boy who asked the question would name a dare—something nasty or hard for the person to do. Adam volunteered to go first to show us how it was done. He sat cross-legged atop a picnic table and waited for the first question. He had my full attention, of course.

"How old are you?" asked Domingo, tentatively.

"Eighteen."

Jose asked, "Do you smoke?"

"I tried it once, but didn't like it. So, no more."

Pedro yelled out, "Do you have a girlfriend?"

Adam hung his head. "Sadly, no."

Pedro yelled again, "Will you come back again after you leave us in August?"

"I don't know."

"Which of us do you like the best?" Alex raised his eyebrows after asking his question.

"Equal. I love you all equally."

Alex said, "Not possible. You owe me a dare!"

Adam responded, "Fair enough. What will it be, Alex?"

"Go to the kitchen and bring me a plantain," he commanded.

"Wait. You know Maria won't let me have anything between meals. She runs a very tight ship."

"A ship?"

"Just an expression. She likes order in her kitchen."

"Well, try hard," said Alex.

Adam pursed his lips, then said, " Okay. I'll try," and headed for the kitchen. A few minutes later he returned without a plantain.

"She said no."

"Did she throw anything at you?"

"No. She just said no and went back to her work. So, boys, since I failed at my dare, my turn is over and I'm a loser. Alex, since you stumped me, you go next."

The boys got Alex to admit he'd kissed a girl but has no girlfriend now. That he planned to work in the tourist industry, and that he didn't want to get married or have children—ever. I wasn't really surprised since I'd heard that a number of the boys weren't technically orphans. Their families brought them because they couldn't care for them. Apparently, some of the parents visited occasionally. I didn't know whether Alex's situation was like that, but even knowing such a thing can happen must do a number on a young boy. So, rejecting the whole scenario of marriage and children wasn't hard to understand. Alex was answering all of the questions, and Adam and I realized his turn could go on forever. So we set a maximum of ten questions. Alex finished all of his with quick, direct answers so he didn't have to do a dare.

I wasn't so lucky. Basic questions like where I was from, family, and school stuff gave me a false sense of security. In addition, I hate being the center of attention. Yet, there I was, sitting on top of a picnic table with everyone looking at me. Then Pedro said, "Are you rich?"

I had to think quickly how to answer. I knew it was a "yes" or "no" question, but "yes" seemed like a terrible answer. So, I said something lame like, "It's always relative, Pedro." I explained that, compared with a Hollywood millionaire, I'm not. But, to a person living off food stamps in a housing project, I would be. They all looked at me like I was speaking Martian, so I just smiled as though I was happy with my answer. Then it got worse.

Alex asked me if I wanted to kiss any of the other volunteers. I said it was an inappropriate question and that I'd neither answer it nor accept a dare. Adam backed me up, but I felt my neck flush and couldn't imagine the boys missed it. Or that Adam missed it. My tell-tale coloring was something I'd inherited from my mom. She'd told me she always wore scarfs or high-necked blouses to work when she had a court appearance, since anxiety and adrenaline showed up on her neck too. I jumped down from my perch on the picnic table and walked over to Domingo. "Would you like to try?" He was so little, and so cute, I knew it would change the dynamic, taking attention off me. It worked. The younger boys lined up for a chance to answer questions, and several tried to elbow their way to the front of the line.

Once they'd each had a turn, we ate a special lunch of hamburgers and hot dogs and then played basketball until the other volunteers got back just before dinner time. As we were leaving the court, Adam leaned over and whispered in my ear, "Stargaze?"

I smiled and nodded.

For our third visit to our spot, the air was almost still. I could hear the hi-pitched whine of the mosquitoes as we made our way up the hill. They were mainly going for my head, and I realized I should've sprayed my hair as well as my face. I swatted at the back of my head and managed to keep them from stabbing me in the scalp. Adam must've covered his whole body with the repellant, since they didn't seem to be landing on him. When we were getting set up at our spot, he reached in his backpack and pulled out the usual blanket and netting, plus two squished up little throw pillows. That explained why, as I'd followed him up the hill, his backpack looked like its seams might burst. When he tossed them to me, I said, "So, if I keep coming up here with you, we'll eventually have a couple of couches?"

He laughed. "Not a bad idea."

After he got the blanket in place and we'd wrapped ourselves in netting, we each grabbed a pillow and sat down. I lay back and made sure my netting covered my entire head, except for a slit for me to see through. Then after Adam did the same, I checked. He was no closer to me than the last time. There was no way I was going to slide nearer to him, since I suspected my romantic interest was much more developed than his…if he had any at all. I definitely didn't want to scare him away by dropping hints about how I felt. I was so excited to be at the beginning of another evening with him and the stars. I took a deep breath of the still air, then said, "Tell me a great myth you think I really should know—even if we can't see the constellation tonight."

He didn't pause to think about it, but immediately said, "Hercules." That made me think he must've been hoping to get to that one, and it would be a good story.

"He's one of the most impressive characters because of his strength and ingenuity. He also makes for one of the largest constellations. But, because it doesn't contain any really bright stars, it is actually hard to see. I will draw him for you tomorrow. Anyway, the myth is that Heracles, well, the Roman name is Hercules, so I'll just use that…."

"Yes. I have to insist on the Latin name."

"So, Hercules was the son of Zeus and a mortal woman."

"Ah. Zeus was cheating on Hera—again!"

"Yes. Not one of his best qualities. Well, when Hercules was a baby, Zeus laid him at Hera's breast while she slept. When she nursed him, he became immortal."

"Wait a minute. Why was Hera lactating if she hadn't also had a baby?"

"I don't know. I never thought about that. But, when Hera found out, she was furious, both at the sneaky nursing trick and at the fact of Zeus's infidelity. She wanted to make Hercules's life as difficult as possible."

"Shouldn't she have wanted to make Zeus' life as difficult as possible? Or, maybe, she thought she could hurt Zeus by hurting Hercules."

"I suppose she wanted to hurt both of them. So she did the worst thing imaginable. She cast a spell on him that made Hercules go insane and kill his own children."

"Oh my. Who could live with himself after that?"

"Yes. It was terrible. Once Hercules realized what he'd done, he travelled to the Oracle at Delphi to find out how he could atone for the horrible deed. The Oracle sent him to a certain king--for twelve years."

"To be his slave?"

"Not exactly. The king started off by assigning Hercules a series of ten incredibly difficult tasks. First, Hercules had to kill a lion, whose skin couldn't be penetrated by any weapon. So, Hercules strangled it, then used its own claw to cut the skin to make a protective coat for himself."

"Clever."

"Yes, I would say so. Second, he had to destroy a many-headed monster. A crab was sent to distract Hercules, but he was able to kill it and the monster. The crab was placed in the sky as another constellation, Cancer. Then, Hercules was required to capture a series of things, all nearly impossible to catch: a deer with golden horns, a destructive fire-breathing bull on the island of Crete, and a ferocious boar."

"My fifth-grade teacher was one of those."

"One of what?"

"A ferocious bore."

"Ha. Good one, Eve. Do you want to hear the rest?"

I thought it was very cool that a German-speaker could so easily catch an English pun. I doubted I could've caught a Latin pun…if they even made them. "Of course, I do. But, first, I have a question. Isn't this basically an elaborate obstacle course, with death as the penalty if Hercules messes up on a single obstacle?"

"Basically."

"Wow. And all from his emotional torture over killing his kids." I tried to think what poor Hercules must've felt like, but my imagination couldn't stretch that far.

"Yes. For him it was unbearable."

"You know, Adam, I think I might be like that. Death wouldn't be so scary if every day was a living hell over something terrible I'd done."

"I can see that, too. The problem is that, since I don't have superhuman strength, I would end up dead, for sure."

"Me too. But on the positive side, our sadness would be over."

"There is something wrong with that, Eve. Are you saying

suicide would be a good way to end sadness?"

"No. I'm just saying I think I'd do anything and everything I could think of to end it. Who'd want to live every day under that kind of cloud?"

"Well, hopefully, neither of us will ever have to face that."

"Yeah. Hopefully." Adam remained quiet, so I added, "So, what else was Hercules assigned to do?"

"He also had to kill a whole flock of terrifying birds, clean the disgusting stables of another king, and fetch certain flesh-eating horses. Then he had to bring to the king the belt off the Queen of the Amazons. Once Hercules arrived at his tenth task, stealing cattle from a monster, he thought he was home free. But local forces attacked him and had almost beaten him. So Hercules prayed to Zeus, who helped him by sending him rocks. Hercules knelt and defeated the enemy by throwing rocks at them."

"So he was finally redeemed?"

"Not quite. When he returned, the king unfairly added on two more tasks. First, Hercules had to steal the golden apples from Hera's garden on Mt. Atlas. The gardens were guarded by Atlas' daughters, and they were guarded by a dragon. The dragon got killed in the process, and Hera, herself, placed it in the sky. The constellation Draco."

"Can we see Draco?"

"Yes. It kind of wraps around the side of the Little Dipper." He pointed. "Just there."

I looked, but I'm not sure I was focused on the right stars. "And Hercules? What was his twelfth task?"

"The last was the hardest. He had to travel to the Underworld and return with the three-headed guard dog. Hercules dragged the dog to the king, who now had no choice but to release Hercules from his pain."

"Well, thank goodness. He really had to earn it. So, did it all came out well for Hercules?"

"No. There's more to the story, Eve."

"Figures."

Adam chuckled. "Hercules finally found his love, and they married. But many years later, when she became suspicious that Hercules was attracted to another woman, she smeared a special poison on a shirt she gave to him. As soon as he realized it was burning through his flesh, Hercules built his own funeral pyre and lay on it to die. His mortal part burned, but his immortal side joined the other gods on Mount Olympus. It was Zeus who placed Hercules in the sky as the constellation."

"Quite a story, Adam. Doesn't reflect terribly well on the jealous wife though."

"That is true. And a bit of a theme. But, remember, the myths were created by men."

"Of course they were. And it explains a lot. It's always about perspective, isn't it?"

"Very often, I think."

As usual, once we'd finished talking about the constellations, he said, "Time to stargaze?"

"Definitely." By that point, I knew I'd have to work at distracting myself from Adam. I decided to review all the constellations to see how many I could remember and find. I also noticed that the sky was so full of stars I could've searched it forever without looking at the same one twice. The sky from that hilltop was an entirely different thing than the one in Chicago. It occurred to me that we really shouldn't even use the same word for them. The one that entranced me that night should be "the firmament" or "the heavens," or something like that. "Sky" wasn't a big enough word.

Leaving heaven was just as hard as the other two nights. I had such mixed feelings, knowing I would have only two more full days in paradise. I wished I could be like Adam's Aunt Bertha and just appreciate what I had.

Chapter 6

The following day, we were supposed to take our boys to visit the English Institute, a trip each group got to make one afternoon a week. They'd be able to choose books from the library there for practice reading. The fact we'd stop for ice cream cones on the way home guaranteed lots of enthusiasm.

I'd only seen the lights of the town center from the window of the bus that brought me, in the pitch dark. It turned out to be about a mile walk from the orphanage. Adam led the way and I brought up the rear so we wouldn't lose any strays. There were sidewalks, but the concrete was pretty broken up, making them more of a tripping hazard than the dirt roads. The problem with the roads was the apparent lack of traffic rules. Small, loud, motorcycles swarmed everywhere like a rush of bees. They zipped around, taking any random route that narrowly avoided head-on collisions. Many of the adults had several children, even babies, lined up in front of them on the motorbikes. There was no way I was going to let one of the boys get mowed down by a speeding Yamaha, so I insisted they walk on the crumbling sidewalk.

The houses we passed were small, mainly cinderblock, with no glass in the windows. Many were painted bright turquoise or salmon. The tiny front yards were basically dirt, and washers and dryers were sitting in the side yards of several of the homes. The people we passed all yelled greetings or gave us big smiles. The boys had on purple t-shirts like ours, so they were clearly from the orphanage. Carmelo taught me to respond with, "Bueno!" and I sincerely hoped it was an appropriate word. An ant colony caught his attention. When he kicked it, the ants skittered in every direction, and he and Domingo ran around in circles trying to step on them. I grabbed both boys by their shoulders, and said, "No! Don't do that."

Domingo looked up at me with his huge brown eyes and asked, "Why not?"

"Because, boys, everything that's living wants to keep living. You wouldn't want a giant to walk down this street and step on you, would you?"

They both giggled and said, "No way!"

The English Institute was a pleasant surprise, with blue and white tiled walls and a small, lush garden. Although it was probably eighty-five degrees and sunny, we were cooled by the shade in the garden and then by overhead fans in the building. Huge, glassless windows, topped by blue awnings, allowed the breeze, flavored with the sweet aroma of the flowers, to flow from one end of the building to the other. And I was thrilled to discover bathrooms with flushable toilets and faucets delivering hot and cold water.

When we got to the room dedicated to the children's library, we were met by two other volunteers, who'd stayed after working with the last group. So each of us ended up with only two boys to read with. I got lucky and was assigned to cutiepies, Carmelo and Domingo. We searched for really basic, beginner reader books, and found ancient "Dick and Janes" as well as several Dr. Seuss classics.

Once, when I was between books, I looked up and saw Adam working with Alex and Carmen using flash cards. The boys whizzed through them and seemed to revel in showing off for Adam. We weren't supposed to speak any Spanish, but I heard them cracking jokes in Spanish with him. I'm just assuming they were jokes from the reactions. Adam looked so relaxed in that setting, like he was really their older brother who belonged there as much as they did.

When I looked back down at the book Domingo had chosen, I saw that it was another Dick and Jane. From the cars in the pictures, I guessed it was from the 1950s. Carmelo pointed at a word and said, "Dog!"

"Very good!" I said.

Then he pointed at Dick and said, "White!" Well, that threw me. Of course, Carmelo was right. Dick was white. So I just said, "Very good. His name is Dick." I pointed at the letters. "See, D-I-C-K." But I wished for a book about people of color. We had tons of them when I was growing up. And I immediately knew I'd screwed up by not bringing my all-time favorite kids' book, *Children Just Like Me*, for the boys. I tried to think what I could do right then and there with Carmelo and Domingo to make it clear that black or brown skin would be just as great on Dick and Jane. I got an idea.

I pointed at my arm and said, "White." Then I pointed at their arms and said, "Brown." They repeated the color names after me. Then I pointed to all of our arms and said, "Beautiful!"

Domingo just looked for a moment, then tentatively pointed at all of the arms. "Beautiful?"

"Yes! Very good, Domingo."

Carmelo stood at my knees and studied on it. Then he pointed at my pale arm, smiled, and said, "Beautiful."

I said, "Yes," then pointed at his little brown arms and said, "Beautiful!" He beamed at me and, after a moment, repeated, "Beautiful!"

Adam had told me about the color prejudice. As in, lighter was better. I assumed it was really about power, like in the United States. Does anyone really think bland, anemic-looking white skin is actually prettier? Seriously, if we did, why do we bake ourselves in the heat and spray on tans? When I looked up, I saw that Adam had been watching me. Apparently, Alex and Carmen had gone off to find more flash-cards to ace. I smiled and nodded. I also felt embarrassed, for no good reason. I planned to ask him later why there weren't some beginner level books with brown characters. But I guessed I knew the answer. The books were donations, so they were simply whatever happened to be in the donors' libraries.

Carmelo and Domingo and I spent our entire two hours with the books and then got ready to leave with the rest of the group. This was a great chance for the boys to wash their hands well, hopefully encouraged by the treat of warm water and bar soap. Actually, I wasn't sure it would mean as much to them as it did to me. I took the opportunity to luxuriate in washing my face with actual warm water. And I got a thrill out of flushing—something I never would've guessed would feel like such a treat. The wash-up had been a waste of time for the boys though, since we made the stop for ice cream cones. It was the hottest part of the day, and whatever wasn't eaten quickly, dripped over their hands and onto their t-shirts. I'd say, another bad plan. But the boys seemed to have enjoyed the cones enough to make up for the mess.

As we were lining up the boys to head home, Adam came over to me and pulled a piece of paper out of his pocket. He said, "I promised you Hercules." The boys were getting rowdy waiting to start our walk, so I simply slipped it into my pants pocket and said, "Thanks, Adam."

We let the boys lead the way home, and they seemed proud to do it. Adam and I shared a cone, so we had to walk together. The vanilla bean ice cream was the icy kind, rich with flavor from the tiny beads of vanilla, and frozen into a rock, so we had to lick it, rather than taking bites. I surprised myself by actually watching carefully where his tongue had just been, and then licking the ice cream, as casually as I could, in the exact same spots. I couldn't help myself. But I really didn't know how he felt about me. Since Adam was so nice to everyone, I just couldn't be sure.

Once we got near the bottom of the ice cream, I saw Adam glance at me as I took the cone and turned it to the spot he'd just licked. A flicker of a smile made me wonder if he'd caught me and been happy about it. Or amused. That night, I found myself wishing Claire was there with me. She would've known whether Adam really liked me, or whether I was kidding myself because I'd come to adore him.

Chapter 7

By the end of the week I was waking up each morning before the roosters started crowing, anxious to get the day going so I could see Adam. On my ninth day, we had a moment alone before the boys joined us. "I know you leave tomorrow, Eve. I'm sorry we haven't had more time to be together."

"Yeah. I know."

"Will you go with me to our spot tonight?"

"Oh, yes!" I gave Adam a big smile, then immediately regretted it because I didn't want to seem too eager.

I'm pretty sure the day was filled with baseball games, reading time with the boys, and some kind of art project. But what I vividly remember is that it took weeks to get through the day. The time dragged like when I was little and endured the agonizing wait for Christmas morning. And then, like a thunderbolt, we were standing at the orphanage gate.

The walk was gorgeously lit for us by a perfect full moon. The steady, gentle breeze reminded me of the overhead fans at the English Institute. Once we got to our spot, Adam and I agreed to skip the mosquito nets, since there were no insects on patrol for us. We sat on the blanket, cross-legged, facing each other.

He laughed. "There's so much I want to ask you and so little time. I'm afraid we'll have to skip the small talk and get right to the good stuff."

"Sounds good to me."

"So, Eve, what do you believe?"

I squinted at him and said, "Isn't that a little broad?"

"Of course." He smiled. "I am an idiot. What I meant

was, what do you think is the meaning of life?"

"Well, that narrows it down." I fake-frowned. "So, we're going to start with the biggest question, and then move backwards?" I was trying hard to concentrate on our conversation, but the pull of wanting to kiss him kept distracting me.

"It makes sense, doesn't it? I mean, in view of the time restriction."

"I guess. Sure." I took my time to organize my thoughts. I had my ideas, of course, but no one had actually asked me this question before. "I think it has to be love."

"Really? What kind of love?"

"All kinds. Love of God, love between parents and children, families, friends, romantic partners, love for humanity, for nature, even love for a cause."

"So, if you love anyone or anything, you've found the meaning of life?"

"No. I don't think so. I think it has to be true love." I smiled because I believed what I was saying. If Adam thought it was simplistic or naïve, I was still comfortable with it.

He looked directly into my eyes and said, "What does true love mean?"

"I just don't think my definition works unless the love is the real thing. I believe true love means putting the person you love ahead of yourself. Otherwise, it's just affection or appreciation or something like that. Of course, we could put someone else's needs ahead of our own for reasons other than true love—maybe duty, or for a selfish purpose. But to me, the meaning of life is discovering the true love within us. It's not just one time, or one thing. I think we have to spend our whole lives searching our hearts for it."

"It's interesting. Why do you think this is so, Eve?"

"I'm not sure. I suppose true love sort of makes the 'self' disappear in favor of the loved one. It's like overcoming self-ishness is what elevates us to a higher level. By taking our egos out of it, I think we have a chance to really be one with the uni-verse." I stopped and let out a long sigh. "I don't really know. Those are just things I've been thinking about. Does it make sense?"

"Yes. Very much." Adam was looking at me very intently, and I was wondering what he really thought.

"So, what's the meaning of life to you?"

"I subscribe to the philosophy of Eve."

"You're making fun of me. Be serious."

"I couldn't be more serious. Your description fits my thinking very well. The way you speak of it, it seems possible to find--not only once, and not in just one way, but many times and in many ways. Your idea is very beautiful." He paused and whispered, "Like you." He said it so quietly, I wasn't sure I'd really heard it. He continued, "Your idea that love is the answer to the most important question, well, it reminds me of what we were taught in church as children. It went something like this: 'God is love. And he who abides in love, abides in God, and God in him.'"

"Maybe it is the same. I think true love is the most impor-tant thing. It's like it's the fulfillment of our destiny."

"Yes. I think you've hit it on the head. And talking about it out here, on this pristine night, with nothing between us and the universe, well, it actually feels religious. Here, in this place, I feel reverence."

"It is amazing to be here." I looked up at the vast blackness, pierced by a thousand tiny pinpricks of brightness, and one perfect, radiant ball.

"With you."

That snapped my attention back to Adam. "With me?"

"Does that surprise you?"

"Maybe. How exactly do you mean that?"

"Amazing to be with you is, how is it said… 'self-evident'?"

"Well, before I make a fool of myself, let me ask you something."

"Sure." He smiled so tenderly I actually felt a little faint.

"Do you mean with me as friends, or romantically?"

Adam leaned toward me and put his hand behind my head. We moved together slowly until we were kissing. His lips were warm, and almost creamy in their softness. I took in his fresh smell, like he'd just stepped out of a shower, with an overlay of insect repellant, and a hint of perspiration. After a few minutes of his incredibly sweet and gentle kisses, we lay down cocooned together in each other's arms. It felt as though time had moved into slow-motion. I knew, even as it was happening, that nothing would ever be as purely sublime as that night. An eternity of embraces, caresses, delicate kisses of butterflies, and feeling Adam's sweet breath on me.

In a whisper, he asked me if I was protected to have sex. Honestly, at that moment, I didn't care. But I told the truth. "Sorry. But I'm a Virgo."

"What? I thought you said your birthday is in October."

I just looked at him for a moment, and then said, "It is."

"Oh. I understand."

"So, no. Not protected."

He whispered, "I have a condom."

That broke the spell for a moment as I wondered about this boy I felt so intimately connected with but had only known for nine days. I pulled back a little. "You brought condoms on a service trip to an orphanage?"

"Of course not."

"Oh. That's good. So, how do you have one?"

"I ran out today to the little tobacco shop near the English Institute. I did not presume. I just wanted us to have the option."

"Oh." I was just lying there, knowing I was going to have to make a decision.

He spoke softly. "Listen, Eve, it is up to you. You do not need to do this. Especially since it would be your first time. Tonight has already been the best one in my life. I only ask what you want to do."

I closed my eyes for a moment to clear my head so I could think straight. And the truth was obvious. There would never again be a moment quite like this, with a boy quite like Adam. It just isn't how things are done back home--how the boys are back home. I'd probably never see him again. But I knew I wanted my first time to be exactly like this. And, I thought, I will never in a million years regret it. I nodded.

Adam slipped off his t-shirt and then mine, his shorts and then mine. It seemed like we spent hours making out. Or maybe it was minutes. When I stroked his shoulders and felt the beat of his heart through his burning hot chest, and ran my fingertips over his face and neck, I learned a whole new meaning to my sense of touch. As I studied his beautiful face, I saw it was framed by a giant halo of stars.

I had on a cotton sports bra, so I just raised my arms and Adam pulled it out to slide over my breasts and then my head. When he leaned down to pull off his underwear, I quickly pulled mine off as well and kicked them out of the way. We had no cover on top, so we were totally exposed to the man-in-the-moon. My body welcomed Adam's touch until I desired nothing more fervently than to meld myself with him.

But when Adam rolled on top of me, I felt like I was being crushed. I had to say something, so I whispered, "I think you're too heavy for me."

He put his knees aside my hips so I could breathe again, and whispered, "Better?"

"Um-hm." After that there was a rush of movement and breathing and sensation that wasn't like anything I even knew was possible. Then we were both out of breath, our chests rising and falling, not quite in unison.

We spent the rest of our time relaxed, as if all of the stress in our lives had melted away. My body fit perfectly against his, my head resting on his chest or in the crook of his neck. Occasionally, I'd lift my head to give or receive a kiss, or turn it to gaze at the stars. There was no sound but our breathing and the crickets in the distance.

We talked a little. I learned Adam had the time to work at the orphanage because he'd finished gymnasium, German high-school, ahead of schedule. He was pushing himself along a bit. And he looked forward to someday getting to a point where he could help his parents financially—and his brothers.

I answered his questions truthfully, but without the boring details. I'd had a boyfriend freshman year, but not recently. I was also looking forward to college. He already knew I was intrigued by the cell, so I went ahead and told him something I hadn't told my parents yet—that I also wanted to become a doctor--maybe genetics or cancer research.

I had been to heaven with the boy I loved, and now I wanted nothing more than just to be with him. So, when it was time to get ready to head back to the orphanage, I fell into a sea of melancholy that threatened to pull me under at the thought of leaving him the next day. I worked hard to summon the willpower to fight it, and decided to try really hard not to let what was left of our time together be marred by worries of all the future nights without him.

Once we'd dressed, wrapped up our mosquito nets and Adam had stashed his blanket, netting and pillows, he wrapped his arms around me and we had one last kiss under the stars before we walked back down to reality. It was as though he'd saved the warmest, softest kiss for last. When we stepped apart, it felt like we'd been attached by Velcro and someone or something was ripping us apart. A lump in my throat and my racing heart made me fear I'd actually hyperventilate. I couldn't speak. Tears welled up and Adam gently wiped them away with his fingertips. He gave me the sweetest smile, wrapped his arm around my shoulders, and walked with me back down the hill, away from heaven.

The next morning, I longed for a few minutes alone with Adam before time to board the bus for the airport. It was also the departure day for one of the small family groups that had arrived with me. The other family had already left for a beach resort. The morning was clear and the temperature was already near eighty degrees as we finished breakfast. I walked around the boys' table and said goodbye to each one of them since they'd be busy doing activities with the other volunteers at the time I'd board the bus. I could tell they were up to something since the younger ones couldn't quit giggling.

The program director asked those who would be leaving to walk toward the baseball diamond so everyone could see as she presented each of us with a new volunteer t-shirt to take home. When we'd gotten about fifty feet from the picnic tables, a large group of the older boys ran at us with buckets of water and doused us like they were putting out a raging fire. First, I had to catch my breath—the blast of cold water had shocked me. Water was still coming at me and I shrieked like a nine-year-old girl. The boys were all cheering and yelling. I saw out of the corner of my eye that the parents of the family group were trying hard not to show how unhappy they really were about this. Their two daughters laughed and screamed as they tried to shake the water from their long hair.

Unfortunately, it wasn't going to be just one assault. Another group arrived with more buckets. I was completely soaked and shivering, in spite of the warmth in the air. My previously modest, over-sized t-shirt and knee-length baggy pants now stuck to me like a second skin. I saw Adam looking at me and realized that he'd never really seen my figure before—except with his hands.

When the boys finally quieted down, Adam walked over to me with a large beach towel. As he wrapped it around me, he whispered, "You are very beautiful wet." I looked up at him, water dripping onto my face from my hair, and bit my lip. I ached to kiss him. Truth be told, at that moment I felt the strongest craving to make love with him. The boys quickly surrounded us, anxious to tell me this was a custom in their country. Well, usually for birthdays, but they also did it when volunteers left. It did have the benefit of making the goodbyes fun instead of sad. As I stood there, surrounded by the beautiful little boys, with Adam at my side, I was already missing all of them—and I was still there! Adam and I promised to keep in touch by texts and Face Time once he finished his work at the orphanage and got back to Germany. But I knew I'd probably never see him again.

Chapter 8

I arrived at Chicago O'Hare late on a Sunday afternoon, after sitting in airports through three long connections. Of course, I thought of nothing but Adam all the way home. I stared at the Hercules drawing most of the time. It was a simple pencil drawing on a piece of yellow notebook paper--a series of connected dots that made an outline of an upside-down man, with his knees bent, holding a large club over his head. It was the only physical connection I still had with him, or so I thought.

From the airplane window, I could see huge piles of snow around the perimeter, and snow plows working all over the tarmac. My folks met me at baggage claim and I was thrilled to see them. I was also glad they'd remembered my winter coat and boots. I really enjoyed sharing stories about the trip with them, and they seemed to appreciate hearing every little detail. I think they were relieved I'd finally spent some time on service work. It's hard to say exactly why, but I didn't tell them about Adam. I think I just wanted to cherish that privately.

When I walked into my bedroom, it seemed foreign. I liked the apple green, black and yellow bold floral bedspread, and the shiny black desk and chair I vaguely remembered painting. But it felt like someone else's spot. I realized I'd have to grow back into it, and my suburban neighborhood, and, probably, my studies. I'd always hated transitions, and this was going to be a big one.

I couldn't see Claire until the weekend after I got back because she'd spent the last week of break in St. Louis with her cousins. It was our last free weekend before school started that she was able to stop by. When I opened the front door, I was shocked to see that she'd cut her long, jet-black hair and now had a close-cropped haircut with short bangs. She looked great. "Claire, oh my God! You look gorgeous."

She stepped into our foyer and slowly spun around so I could see all the angles. "Thanks. Do you really like it?"

"It's amazing! You look so sophisticated. Where'd you get it done?"

"Basically, it was an accident." She shook the snow from her parka, and hung it on our antique brass coat stand.

"How?"

"Well, I went down to that hoity-toity salon just off Michigan Avenue, where the student stylists do the super cheap cuts." Claire leaned against the wall to pull off her Uggs.

"Yeah. I've heard about it."

"I just asked for a trim. But the girl talked me into getting a precision cut by telling me how my face was perfect for it. Actually, she probably just needed to practice that kind of cut."

"But she was right. It's really flattering. You just look so mature and elegant. You know what?"

"Is there a *but* coming?"

"No! I was just going to say that looking more mature might help you get one of the journalism internships you want for the summer."

"Thanks, Eve. That would be great. My parents are still getting used to it. But I think I really look different. I'm pretty sure I like it." She patted the edges with her fingertips, then turned around again so I could get a good look. We walked upstairs to my bedroom, and Claire plopped down on my shiny black retro beanbag chair. I sprawled out on my bed.

"You know, it's like in all those movies," I said.

"What movies?"

"You remember. The ones my mom always played for us when we were in elementary school. Like *Roman Holiday* and *Sabrina.*"

"Oh, yeah. When the girl cuts her hair, she liberates herself and becomes sophisticated and totally stunning."

"Exactly," I said.

"That's still a thing, you know. Like in that *Joy* movie from a few years ago, about the woman inventor, where Jennifer Lawrence cuts her own hair to do battle with the patent thief. And that really old Melanie Griffith flick…."

"*Working Girl.* I remember." I paused for a few moments to think. "But, Claire, what does it all mean? Is it some guy-fantasy that the really attractive women are actually the strong ones who quit trying so hard with the flowing manes bit, and just chop off the baggage?"

"I don't know. But I think you're giving the director too much credit. Isn't it just a shortcut way to show the transformation of a female character from weak to strong? I mean, other than the actresses' spilling out emotions, all they have to work with is her clothes…maybe the music. I suppose it's kind of a cheat. They should be able to show it with the writing and acting…without needing the cliché chopping off of the tresses."

"Except for one thing, Claire."

"What's that?"

"The short haircuts really do make the actresses more attractive. They're like you. Their faces are just better suited to the shorter cuts."

"Is that a compliment?"

"Of course. Maybe the prettier look for those actresses just happens to be short hair. So, it's not just a gimmick. It's gutsy and it really does make them look more elegant. Who knows? Anyway, you look totally sophisticated."

"Thanks, Eve. That makes me feel better about it. So, how was the DR?"

I sat up, cross-legged, and smiled. I told her about the orphans, and the general set-up, including the mosquito nets and the rooster alarm clocks. And I told her I'd met someone.

"Oh, my God! Is he Dominican?"

"No. German."

"Really?"

"Yeah. He's a long-term volunteer, so he'll be at the orphanage through mid-August. Then he heads back to Germany to work for a couple months before he starts university."

"Oh, my God! You found someone. That's so cool, Eve." She jumped up on my bed to sit across from me. "So, what's his name?"

"Adam."

"You're shitting me."

"What?"

"Seriously? Adam and Eve?"

"It's just his name, Claire. It wasn't a subliminal message I should fall in love with him."

"Fine." Claire laughed. "Well, what's he like?"

"He's wonderful. So sweet with the little boys, and just a natural at everything. Adam is totally different from the guys we know. He has a really level-headed, mature way of looking at things."

"What does he look like?

"Tall. Light brown hair, blue eyes."

"I need more, Eve. Don't you have a picture?"

"I wish I did. We weren't allowed to take our phones."

"Well, that's a lame rule." She frowned. "Okay. Try this. What movie star does he look like?"

I had to think about it for a few minutes, since, to my mind, all movie stars paled in comparison. Finally, I looked at Claire and said, "A young Matt Damon, maybe. Or possibly that Leonardo guy from *Titanic*."

"Very nice."

"Well, he just has that boyish kind of face."

"But not blond?"

"No."

"Good. I was having trouble not seeing him like one of those 'Hitler Youth' pictures from our history books."

"Good God, Claire!"

"Sorry. But those were always handsome, blond boys—so my mind just went there."

"That's stupid."

"Yeah. It is." She added, breathlessly, "So, how'd it happen? What do you know about him? Did you two do anything interesting?"

"Whoa. Slow down. If you really want to know, I'll tell you the whole story...not that it's all that long."

"Are you kidding? My best friend fell in love over Christmas break. That's pretty huge! So yeah, I really want to know."

I told Claire all the details of my days at the orphanage, and my time with Adam. Everything except for the sex. She was so excited for me, but seemed unconvinced Adam could be as wonderful as I described. I couldn't manage to do him justice with mere words. "Well, it was amazing to be with him. But the truth is, Claire, I'll probably never see him again."

"Can't you text or Face Time, or something?"

"Yeah. Once he gets back to Germany. But it won't be the same. I really don't think anything can ever really be quite as perfect as my time with Adam."

"Well, that's harsh. You think you've already had your best romance at age sixteen?"

"Yeah. I really do." I sighed.

"But, Eve, you have to keep in mind that you only knew Adam for ten days."

"So?"

"So, you didn't have time to see his flaws come out. We all have them, you know."

"I know. But that's not his fault."

"No. But it's still pretty unfair to all of the future boyfriends you'll be comparing him with."

"Maybe. But how can I not, Claire?"

"You're so screwed."

"Probably. But I can't help how I feel."

Claire and I went downstairs for food, watched some TV, and gabbed like we hadn't seen each other in a year. A lot of it was about Adam, but not all of it.

Later that day, after she'd left, I began to feel really down. Adam was gone. But I could still feel his presence, like what I'd read about the phantom pain after an amputation. Talking about him with Claire had made me miss him even more.

And then I was back in school, with a tremendous amount of homework. It was almost as though, in this last year and a half of high school, they were trying to cram in everything I'd ever need to know. Of course, the AP classes were the most demanding. But I told myself there was no way I could become a doctor if I couldn't ace my bio class. We were starting a chapter called Genetic Engineering: A Revolution in Molecular Biology. I was loving it, but it stretched me beyond what I was used to. Sometimes I visited my teacher with questions, since I was trying hard to keep on track. I'd never had to do that before. Labs were the best part, and really helped me understand the books. Looking through the microscope, I was able to start to get concepts that I couldn't quite grasp in lectures or studying on my own. But what absolutely transported me was the sheer beauty of what I saw on the slides. It confirmed for me that my first impulse had been right. This was exactly what I wanted to do with my life.

***

A week later, Claire and I were hanging out in my bedroom, studying for a Latin test. I happened to mention my period was a couple of days late. I'd seen just a tiny bit of spotting about a week before. But, I told her I knew travelling can mess you up that way. When I mentioned later that my boobs were achy she said, "Could you be pregnant?"

I laughed and told her of course not. After all, I knew I'd had sex only one time, and Adam had used a condom. I remembered from health class that they're 98% effective if used exactly right, and otherwise, they're 85% effective. Pretty good odds...especially if Adam had used it "exactly right." And, from what I'd seen, he did everything exactly right.

She said something like, "Oh, good. I had to ask because

my cousin got really achy boobs when she was pregnant. Plus, the area around her nipples turned dark." I laughed again, but I was distracted after that. The thing was that mine were darkening. Once she left, I went on-line to look at the symptoms of pregnancy. I definitely had the fatigue, but who isn't worn out after a big trip? And I had to pee a lot, but only a little more often than usual. Still, I was worried about what Claire had said.

I told Mom I needed some tampons and ran out to the drug store. Once I found the pregnancy tests, I looked around to make sure no one I knew was in the store. Then, as an extra precaution, I grabbed a magazine to set on top of it at check-out. Fortunately, the older Indian man who rang me up didn't seem to have any interest in what I was buying, or for whom. When I got back to my room I read the instructions twice. I couldn't afford to do something wrong and have to go back to the drug store since I would die of embarrassment.

I went downstairs and drank a giant glass of orange juice to be sure I'd have enough urine. The test was going for something called my "mid-stream," and I'd never had to locate that part before. Then I went back upstairs and tried to work on homework for a half hour until I felt I'd explode if I didn't pee. Sitting on the pot, with the door locked, I held the strip in my right hand and relaxed. After the stream seemed to be at a reasonably likely mid-point, I put the strip in and then removed it. Almost immediately, I saw the line. It was positive.

I couldn't understand. How could this happen? I'd bet my life on odds that good. I suppose I had. Jesus. Still, I couldn't get my head around it. It was as though that girl on the toilet wasn't really me--just a drama I was watching on TV. I swallowed hard and tried to slow my heart rate with deep breathing.

I'd planned on having children one day--at least two. A pregnant woman always struck me as a special creature, walking around among the rest of us as though she were like us. Of course, she isn't like us at all, because she's the host of nature's miracle. She'll shortly give us a whole new human--a perfectly innocent one with unlimited potential. I'd always thought of pregnancy as really beautiful—never as a problem, and certainly not my problem. But it was, and a big one. My mind was racing, but my body felt nothing but nervous agitation and an urge to barf. There was no way I could think this through alone. I grabbed the strip, instructions and packaging and stuck it all into a plastic bag. I'd have to throw it away somewhere other than home. I quickly washed my hands and threw cold water on my face to put out the fire.

When I called Claire to come over, she said, "I just left an hour ago."

"I know. But I have something important to tell you."

"Why didn't you tell me when I was there?"

"I didn't know then. I ran out to the drug store right after you left."

"Oh, shit." She paused. "I'll be right there."

Chapter 9

Claire ran in the front door without knocking and zipped up
the stairs to the landing, where I was waiting for her. She gave
me a big, snowy hug. Then, while she threw her coat and boots
on my floor, and I blotted the melting flakes on my sweatshirt
with a tissue, she asked to see the evidence. I showed her my
pee-stick and she read the instructions and agreed it was clear.
We sat down on my bed, cross-legged, to talk. "But when?"

"I didn't tell you I slept with Adam because I just wanted
to keep it for myself."

"I get that. But what are you gonna do? You know, it'll just
keep growing in you like a tumor if you don't do something."

I wondered if it was even possible to say it worse. But I
just inhaled really deeply and said, "I know." I'd taken the long
breath to keep from crying. It didn't work. I grabbed a throw
pillow and crumbled into it, my sobs rolling over each other. I
was starting the next one before the last one ended. Claire put
her arms around me, but it was no use. I didn't stop crying until
my eyes ran out of tears.

"Oh my God, Eve. Are you okay?"

"Of course not."

"What can I do?"

"Nothing." I was wiping my face on the bottom of my
sweatshirt and desperately needed a tissue. "Kleen-x?"

Claire grabbed a box from my dresser and I blew until I
could breathe through my nose again.

"You know, Eve, this doesn't have to be a huge deal."

"Oh, right. It's hardly worth talking about."

"Come on. I just mean there's nothing stopping you from

getting a quickie abortion. Will your folks help you?"

"I doubt it. My mom's pro-life, so this'll hit her really hard."

Claire raised her eyebrows. "No kidding? She seems like she'd be a big feminist."

"She is. She just doesn't agree with abortion."

"Is that really possible?"

"Of course it is. I just told you my mom's a pro-life feminist."

"Well, that's bad. You know, you need proof you've told a parent."

"Yeah. I know." I grabbed a magazine off my night stand and fiddled with it.

"Maybe we could find an abortion doc who wouldn't insist on the proof. Then you'd never even have to tell your parents."

"I don't see it, Claire. Why would a doctor want to risk his license that way?"

"To help you. Duh! And you've probably got enough money saved from your summer jobs."

"It's for school."

Claire looked at me like I was nuts. "Eve, remember this equation: little baby equals no college."

"I don't know."

"You just cried your eyes out for like five minutes. Don't tell me you're even thinking of having the baby."

"I said I don't know because I don't know."

"Seriously? You don't want to make the problem disappear—easy-peasy?"

"It's not just a problem, Claire. It's also a living being."

"Yikes." She actually threw her arms up. "If you start

thinking like that, you're in real trouble."

"I am in real trouble."

Claire said, "You are pro-choice, aren't you?"

"Of course. But…." I cleared my throat.

"What 'but'?"

"But it's a hell of a lot easier to stand up for some other woman's right to do what she wants with her body. I promise you, Claire, if you were pregnant, you'd be conflicted too."

"Maybe. But I doubt it. You know I'm very practical."

"I know. You're the most unsentimental person I know."

She smiled like it was a big compliment. "Thanks. So, I'd probably try not to think about the cute little embryo and just look at it as a mole-removal or something. As long as I didn't focus on it, I don't think it would screw up my psyche or anything."

I was having trouble believing she could be so nonchalant about it. I rolled my eyes. "That's your advice? Do it mindlessly?"

"Yeah. It is. Look, if you think too much about it, it'll be harder to pull the trigger."

"I'm not gonna shoot it."

"You know what I mean. You have to dive in without thinking about it or you'll make it a lot harder on yourself."

"You know, Claire, a minute ago I said I was pro-choice."

"Yeah."

"Well, that's not the same thing as pro-abortion. I still have to do the choice part."

"Really?" She looked genuinely puzzled.

"Yeah. Listen, if you were pregnant right now, don't you think you'd want to weigh all the pros and cons?"

She waited a few seconds and then said emphatically, "No."

"Why the hell not?"

"Because a junior in high school, who's already aced the ACT and can go to practically any college she wants, has no business having a baby. Think what it'll be like. The baby would be born somewhere at the beginning of our senior year. By then, you'd be huge. And our class hasn't exactly distinguished itself for being kind."

"I know."

"And social media will devour you for breakfast."

"I know. I'll have to keep myself from looking, so I don't kill myself."

She nodded. "If anyone could pull that off, it's you. But how will you ignore the looks at school?"

"I could rub hot coals in my eyes to blind myself."

"Brilliant. I can get you some from my dad's Weber." She bounced up and started pacing around my room, fidgeting with the zipper on her sweater.

"Thanks. So, do you think the school would still let me be president of NHS next year?"

"No. I can't really see that happening."

"Crap."

She stopped and looked at me hard. "Yeah. But as horrible as that would all be, Eve, the pregnancy actually would be the easy part. Then you either have to give it up—which I can't see you doing—or spend the next eighteen years of your life raising it. And how, exactly, are you going to pay for a baby with the minimum wage job you'll be stuck in if you don't go to college? Like I said, I'm just being practical." She added that the so-called baby was smaller than the eraser at the end of a pencil, and I was overthinking it.

"Listen, Claire, I really appreciate your advice—and I'll think about what you said. It's just too new. I have to think it through. Like you said earlier, you *are* practical. But you know how I have to really dissect things—how I think through every detail before I make a move. There's no way I can stop myself from doing that with the biggest decision I've ever had to make."

"I know. I won't harp at you about it—for awhile. Just let me know when you want my excellent advice again."

I laughed. "Sure thing. Thanks for coming back over right away."

"Are you kidding? How could I not?"

I felt exhausted and assumed Claire would take off at that point. But, she stayed sitting on my bed, just staring at me with a Cheshire cat smile.

I laughed. "What?"

"Are you up for talking about it?"

"About what?"

"You know. What was sex like?"

"Oh, Claire." A wave of calm washed over me. "I'd love to talk about that night."

"Great! So, how was it?"

"Wonderful."

"Really? It didn't hurt at all?"

"Oh no. It was heaven."

Claire huffed. "Well, that just confirms my suspicion that most of us had our hymens broken years ago during gymnastics or using a tampon or something."

"Yeah. I guess. Honestly, Claire, I can't imagine anything will ever be that wonderful again."

"I'm glad it was great. But you're sixteen, Eve. I really think there'll be lots of sex in your future." She actually patted my hand, which felt a little maternal.

"Maybe."

"So, how many times did you guys do it?"

Her question bothered me. Like she thought we were sex maniacs or something. "Just once, Claire. Just one time."

"Wow. I didn't even know you were thinking about getting laid in the DR."

"I wasn't. And I didn't 'get laid'. That sounds so passive. I can't explain it. But, honestly, nothing I've read about it or seen in movies even comes close."

"I still don't get it. What was so great?"

I tried to explain the combination of Adam and the sur- roundings, but I couldn't do it justice. "Maybe it was because we weren't just having sex; we were making love."

Claire was listening, but she didn't speak for a while. Then she said, "So, did he say he loved you that night?"

It's funny. I hadn't thought about that before. He definite- ly did not use those words. I said, "Not exactly. But it definitely felt like he did."

"Say it?"

"No. Feel it. He just looked at me like he loved me."

"Can you tell me any of his really good lines?"

"What do you mean?"

"You know. What romantic things did he say?"

I told her I wanted to keep it private, but generally, he'd mentioned the way I worked with the boys, and my sense of humor.

"It sounds like a performance evaluation at work."

I laughed. "It didn't feel that way. Anyway, the words lovely and compelling and beautiful were in there somewhere." I admitted I couldn't explain Adam. That it was almost as though he'd been an apparition. He was exactly what I'd have come up with if I'd been invited to imagine my ideal boy.

She hugged me. "Well then, I'm glad he was worth all the shit you're about to go through."

"Yeah. He really was." Tears pooled in my eyes again, but I used the back of my hand to smear them away.

"Hey. I didn't mean to make you sad again."

"It's okay, Claire. It's not you." I slid off the bed and stood up for a big stretch. "I'm wiped out. Can I just call you tomorrow?"

"Of course." She jumped into her coat and boots, gave me a big hug, and sprinted back down the stairs. As I heard the door close behind her, I realized I'd have to decide for myself what to do. And I just didn't know. I lay back down on my bed to think.

The fact is, my parents and I are really close. I've heard that happens a lot with only-children. I would've given anything not to have to drag them through it. But I just couldn't do it-- I had to tell them. But not yet. I needed to do some kind of analysis. Even if they wouldn't agree with it, I knew they'd appreciate it if I'd thought it through.

Chapter 10

I knew a little bit about how the cells get together during conception because Mom and Dad used in vitro fertilization, IVF, to conceive me, and Mom told me all about it. She'd always been generous with information about the facts of life. I'd often thought she'd been a little too generous, but now I appreciated knowing. They used to call people like me "test-tube babies." But these days, it's so common that how a lady got pregnant isn't even discussed. My parents were thirty-nine when they decided to go with IVF.

She said they'd been trying for like ten years and all of a sudden, it was now or never. Mom had endometriosis, which means that tissue like the lining of her uterus grew in her fallopian tubes and ovaries. So, first she took drugs to get rid of that, then waited four months and started the IVF drugs.

Basically, the IVF drugs made her ovaries release more eggs. Finally, Dad had to inject a drug into her bottom with a long needle. That part must've been hard since he sometimes faints at seeing blood. (Maybe that's why he became a psychiatrist.) Mom was the worst patient in her IVF group—only three eggs. That had to have hurt since she's very competitive. Also, if she'd produced more, she could've had the extra ones frozen for the future. That way she wouldn't have had to go through all the drugs and the egg retrieval the next time she tried.

Anyway, her three eggs were removed by a needle through the walls of her vagina and uterus, but two of the eggs weren't quite right. The only good one, me, was fertilized in a Petrie dish with my dad's sperm. Actually, in my case, a nice normal looking sperm was chosen and injected directly into the egg. That was how I got started. Not too romantic, but I'm here. Within a few hours, embryo-me became zygote-me. By day 6, I'd become a Blastocyst, meaning I began to differentiate into two types of cells. Labs usually like to grade the Blastocysts and put the best one into the mom's womb. Hard to believe I was already being graded. They had to pick me though, since I was the only one.

A fine tube was placed through her cervix and into Mom's uterus and I got squirted into the cavity. The uterus isn't really a big open space like some textbooks show it. Actually, the two walls are pressed tightly together. It's sticky in there and it has a lot of little folds. So I stuck just fine.

They were both forty when I was born. They tried again a year later but Mom didn't have any decent eggs left. Their story has always made me feel like I might be smart to freeze some of my eggs as soon as I start a real job and can afford it. I'm a big believer in an ounce of prevention. Based on Mom's experience, I've never taken my fertility for granted. Well, now I guess it's not something I have to worry about. Apparently, I'm as fertile as Mom's beloved rich, black garden soil. So fertile I can conceive through a condom.

Being a science geek, I wanted to check out the details of what was happening in my body. It was a good distraction from having to make *the big decision*. I had the advantage of knowing exactly when I'd had sex, January 10th. Well, I thought that was an advantage until I started reading up on it. Actually, the books say they measure your due date, and everything along the way, from an artificial Day 1—the first day of your last period. Which meant that you could have had two of your weeks of pregnancy done before you even had sex. Weird. For me, Day 1 was December 27th. I'm like clockwork. I mean, I was. So, now I could work it out from either date. I just had to be clear on which point they were measuring from. Based on the artificial Day 1, my due date was October 4th.

I learned a lot. Embryo size was especially interesting to me because, if I decided to abort, I'd feel a lot better about it if it's the size of a pea than the size of a baby doll. On the day I told Claire, I was at the beginning of week 5, so the embryo was the size of an orange seed. At week 7, it's like a blueberry; and by week 8, a large raspberry. The fruit-based sizing goes on from there. Week 9, it's like a medium green olive. Wait. Is an olive even a fruit? Anyway, at week 10, it's called a fetus, and it's the size of a prune. By week 12, the size is like a small plum, and it's peach-sized by week 13.

I thought all of those sizes were pretty small and insignificant. It was the developmental stuff I read that shocked me. Pretty amazing. Since I was at week 5, its heart was already beating. By week 7 its mouth and tongue are forming, and its arm and leg buds. Also, the kidneys are already set to begin making urine. By week 9 we should be able to hear its little heartbeat with a special listening device. Now, that's the kind of thing that might make this feel real. Toenail and fingernail beds and teeth buds are forming at week 10. At week 11 it has "human characteristics." By the end of week 12, although just plum-sized, most of its systems are fully formed. And the baby's vocal cords are developing during week 13, the official end of the first trimester.

I didn't look beyond that because, if I got an abortion, I planned to do it before that, since it's totally legal until then.

The couple of days I'd spent studying cell development had been a relief. It was fascinating. After all, it was science, my favorite thing to study. But somehow, I still couldn't really imagine that stuff happening inside me.

I knew I also needed to understand how a first trimester abortion is done. Were there any choices I could make? I was in the middle of an article on medication abortions when Mom knocked on my door as she walked in to hand me a magazine which had come in the mail for me. I slammed down the top of my laptop. She just stared at me. I've never been quick on my feet, so I said something lame like, "Whew! I just finished an essay for school." Then I made an overly big smile and added, "A great time to relax with my new *Vogue*. Thanks, Mom."

She sort of squinted at me, then said, "Listen, sweetie, I have to run downstairs to the office to take a conference call. So don't use the landline for a while."

"I never do," I said. Then I made a too-big smile again.

After reading a number of articles and watching several short videos, I felt I understood first term abortions in a basic way. First of all, nature ends one out of five pregnancies by miscarriage. When women do have abortions, over 90% of them are in the first trimester. Over 20% of those are the medication abortions I'd been reading about when Mom walked in. I would take a pill which would tell my body to shed my uterine lining, and my embryo would go out along with it. The drugs are supposed to be given under a doctor's supervision. But, apparently, women are now getting the drugs in ways that fly under the radar for their do-it-yourself abortions. This method can only be used up to week 10.

The most common way to abort during the first trimester is by some sort of suction machine. Up to 7-week pregnancies can be ended by a "manual vacuum aspiration." A thin tube would be inserted into my uterus, and the embryo would be sucked out when the doctor works the manual pump. It's even more common, though, for the doctor to use a "dilation and electric suction," which is more powerful, and louder, and can be done at up to 16 weeks. For this procedure, my cervix would need to be dilated—opened up. That would be done by the insertion of a series of skinny rods, then larger and larger ones, until my cervix was open wide enough. I could only pray I'd be unconscious if anyone ever did that to me. The doctor would use a straw-like tube, basically a miniature vacuum cleaner. He would switch on the pump, and then sweep the tube around inside my uterus until all of the embryo-stuff was removed. He might also use a loop-shaped spoon called a curette to be sure that all the embryo parts have been scraped out. With both of the suction abortions, the doctor would have to rinse off everything he's removed and then examine it to make sure nothing was left in me. The doctor wouldn't want to mess up by leaving something behind that shouldn't be in there, since I could get an infection. I have to admit, it did make my stomach feel a little sick to think about some doctor lining up a teeny-tiny head and teeny-tiny limbs to make sure he'd gotten it all.

I'm not usually squeamish, which I think should come in handy if I do get into med school. But it was totally more fun to read about a baby's development than about how abortions are done. Unfortunately, neither learning about embryo development, nor how abortions are done really helped me decide which way to turn. I realized I needed to go a different direction and try to evaluate the morality of my choices. I thought about all of the pros and cons I could imagine for each option. But now I wonder how that ever helps anybody decide anything. So, at the end of week 5, I was no closer to a decision.

I knew I was going to have to bite the bullet and tell my parents. I decided to call Claire first. I eased into my beanbag chair and looked out at the gray sky as I rang Claire's cell. She answered on the first ring. "Hi, Claire. Good time to talk?"

"Yeah. Great! I was just thinking about you. Well, the truth is, I've been thinking about your situation since you told me."

"Any new bright ideas?"

"Just the same one I already gave you."

"You seriously have no interest in the baby's point of view?"

"No. I don't. And the people who are pro-life are usually just following the orders of some church, led by old white guys who don't really give a shit about the woman."

"I told you. My Mom's pro-life."

"So?"

"So, she's agnostic. And her thought process isn't based on anything from the old, white guys. Also, she practically tithes for Planned Parenthood."

"Seriously? As in, ten percent of her income?"

"I'm not sure. But she's a big financial supporter."

"But, Eve, they do abortions."

"She knows. She just wants to support the family planning stuff. Helping young women get birth control is really important to her...ironically. Anyway, I just think the way my mom looks at it shows that a woman can be enlightened about contraception, and still be pro-life."

"Eve, even if I agreed with that—which I'm not sure I do—where does that lead us?"

I grabbed a teen magazine from a pile on my floor and started flipping between the same two pages without seeing them. "I just think it means it's not unreasonable for me to consider having the baby."

"Yes, it is. Under the circumstances."

"Claire, stop. I really want to talk with you about this. Can you at least think it through with me?"

"Actually, I've been thinking about it nonstop."

"So, have you come up with anything better than mindlessly aborting?"

"Yeah. I have. Here's what I think. It's bullshit you have to go through this. It makes me so mad that a woman has to either abort the embryo—which could probably scar her for life; or carry it for nine months and then give it away—which could definitely scar her for life; or raise it--which would completely change her entire life. And, probably not for the better."

"Well, that's just the way it is."

"I know. I was just wishing that some clever scientist would come up with a way that this shit couldn't happen."

"What could that possibly be, Claire?"

"Well, this is kinda futuristic. But, I'm imagining a pill that girls start taking at puberty. It prevents periods and the possibility of getting pregnant until the woman actually wants to try for a baby. Then she takes another pill and her period starts up so she can get pregnant. Now, why in the world aren't the brilliant scientists working on that?"

"I like it, Claire. No more nasty periods, and no more

surprise babies."

"Exactly. I'm talking about eliminating all unwanted pregnancies."

"It's a great idea. When I'm a scientist, I promise to work on it."

"Except that you'll never be a scientist if you have a baby in high school."

"It'll be harder, for sure. Unfortunately, I didn't get that pill at puberty, and I am pregnant. A minute ago, you described all my options as bad."

"They are."

"But you still want me to choose the only one that would also be terminally bad for the baby."

"Embryo."

"Okay. Embryo.

"Yeah. I do."

"Fine. Your preference is noted."

Claire tried another approach. "So, what does Adam think? Surely, he agrees with me."

"I haven't told him." I felt embarrassed to say those words, which was probably a clue that I was blowing over something important.

"Really?"

"Yeah. I could probably reach him using the emergency number at the orphanage. But I don't want him to have to worry about this. I mean, it's not like he was careless. He used a condom. We just happened to be in the unlucky two percent."

"But don't you think he'd want to know you're carrying his baby?"

"Well, Claire, what are his options if he knows?"

"The usual ones. Urge you to have an abortion or to keep the baby and he'll contribute to its support."

"Actually, I don't think he or his family has much money. But he's so honorable, he'd probably say that whatever I want to do is fine with him. Then, if I have the baby, he'd do something ridiculous like drop out of school so he could make money to help me. He wants to be a doctor."

"So do you."

"I know. But I have resources and he doesn't. The last thing I want to do is deprive the world of a dedicated doctor."

"Like yourself?"

"Stop, Claire. I get your point. My bottom line is that I don't want to tell him. Maybe someday." I tossed the magazine in the corner.

"Whatever. But has it occurred to you that you aren't telling him because you know he'll want you to have an abortion?"

"I hadn't really thought about it like that. But, maybe… subconsciously. I just know I don't want to tell him yet. Okay?"

"Sure. Whatever. So, you're going to tell your folks tonight?"

"Tonight."

"Good luck."

"Thanks. I'll keep you posted."

"Definitely. I'm here to help."

Chapter 11

I waited until dinner was over since I knew none of us would feel much like eating after I'd told them. Of course, I could only nibble at mine, but they didn't seem to notice. Once I saw they'd both finished their meals, I said something like, "I've got something to tell you guys." They both looked up, I'd say expectantly. Like it was going to be good news—the kind I usually brought home from school, at least in academics.

I hemmed and hawed for a while until Dad said, "Eve, just say it. It can't be that bad."

"It can, actually. But I do have to say it. So, here goes." I paused. "I'm pregnant."

They looked at each other, but neither of them spoke. It was as though that was the very last thing they'd expected to come out of my mouth, and their minds were racing to catch up with my words. I'm sure they weren't just staring at me to make me uncomfortable, but it really did. "Come on. Somebody say something."

They both pushed their plates away and looked at me. "But how could you be pregnant?" said Mom. "You're not even dating." As though this fact could reverse what I'd just said. Mom did keep pretty close tabs on my social life and I got the impression she was absolutely fine with me not dating.

"I know."

"Well then," said Dad, "what's going on?"

I had never had trouble talking with my parents before, but my mouth dried up like a desert. I said, "I need some water," took several gulps from my glass, and then just sat there.

"Sweetie," said Mom, "your father asked you what's going on. We can't help you if you don't talk to us about it."

Something about how nice they were being made me feel like they were somehow hoping that I'd been taken advantage of. "You mean, when did I get pregnant?"

"I'm looking for when, where, with whom, and, for God's sake, why?" said Mom. I noticed the five "w" words made a neat alliterative sentence. The additional "how," which Claire told me she learned in journalism class is so important, was unnecessary.

"Sure. Those are fair questions." They continued staring at me. "Okay, so it was at the orphanage, with one of the other volunteers."

Mom sucked in her breath.

Dad said, "What's his name?"

I started to answer but realized they'd have no way to find out. There'd been probably a dozen other male volunteers my age and a half-dozen counselors. And I knew I didn't want Adam dragged into it. Not yet anyway. I sighed. "I just know his first name. And I'd rather not say."

"Well, if you want to keep living here, you'll say," said Dad. I already thought he'd blame it on Adam. This kinda confirmed it.

Mom jumped in. "I'm not sure how we'll ever get through this if our first reaction is to kick Eve out of the house."

"You know that wasn't my point, Jennifer. But I think it's perfectly reasonable to have the boy's name."

"Of course, Dan. But let's save the threats at this point."

Dad looked up at the ceiling as though he were being forced to talk with a couple of fools.

Mom's inner lawyer kicked in and she started acting very cool, asking me one question after the other. "How far along are you?"

"I'm starting week 6."

"Why did you keep this from us?"

"I've only known for six days myself and I've been trying to figure it out."

"What did you manage to figure out?"

"That I don't know what to do."

"Who else knows?"

"Only Claire."

"Why did you tell her?"

"She's my best friend. And I thought she might be able to help me decide what to do."

"What did she say?"

"That it's crazy for me to stay pregnant at this point in my life, and I should try to sneak out and get an abortion without telling you guys."

Mom said, "Oh. Great friend!" Dad nodded.

"Mom, she was only trying to protect me. She really thought that would be the best thing."

"What did you think of her advice?"

"I'm here, aren't I?"

"Did you think about the possibility of pregnancy before you had sex?"

"Of course."

"So you used protection?"

"Yes. Condom."

"He brought it? Or them?"

"Yes. It." Her question annoyed me, just like when Claire asked it. "Jeez, Mom, it was just one time."

Mom paused and Dad jumped in. "Have you thought

about how impossible this is? If you have this baby, you'll ruin your life."

"Dad, I've thought about my life, and it would make a huge change to every single plan I have. If I have the baby, my life will be ten times as hard. Probably worse than that. But this is on me. I don't want it to affect your lives." Dad just groaned.

"Have you thought about placing the baby for adoption?" asked Mom.

"Yeah, I have, Mom. I don't think I could do it. I would love the baby too much. I think my choices are to change every single thing in my life or to have an abortion."

"Then how can it even be a question? The problem's easily solved," said Dad.

Mom shot back, "For whom?"

"For Eve, of course."

"And what about the life she carries in her? I'd say abortion will be way more than ten times as bad for him or her. Don't you think, Dan?"

"Jesus, Jennifer. This is your daughter's life we're talking about."

"And our grandchild's." She stared at him and he looked away.

Mom looked so sad, I jumped in to help her. "Dad, what if I only have one good egg, like Mom? What if this is it?"

He didn't say anything.

Mom turned to me. "You need to be involved in the decision, Eve."

"No kidding," I said.

She smiled at me. "What I mean is, in this state, you can get an abortion without our consent, as long as we know you're doing it. But we expect to be involved in every step of this thing."

"That's fine."

"So, we'll figure this out as a family."

Dad said, "But what your mother and I say goes."

"Well," said Mom, "maybe we'll all agree, so let's not go there yet, Dan." I was fairly certain we weren't all going to agree.

Mom made it sound very simple. "Eve, tomorrow, I'll give you three books to read which are unabashedly pro-life. I've read a lot of philosophy and ethics texts, and I'll give you three of the best—very readable. And, Dan, if you want to, please give Eve three of the most persuasive books you can find which support abortion in this situation." I knew Mom's selections were likely to be more carefully chosen than Dad's, since she reads both pro-life and pro-choice stuff all the time. Then again, Dad's no slacker. I liked Mom's plan. After all, we had to do something to get beyond what was clearly a tie vote for them. As for me, I was every bit as uncertain as the day I took the pee test. I started to clear the table, but Mom said she'd do it—that I should go upstairs and try to relax. I gave them each a hug and retreated, as fast as I could, up the stairs.

Unfortunately, they went into the family room after I'd gone into my bedroom. It wasn't like I didn't want them to know I could hear voices from there. It was just that they hadn't had another real argument since the one about the Women's March, three years before. Also, this issue was serious enough that I wanted to know their real feelings, even if it was underhanded. I sat, motionless, on the corner of my bed.

Dad started with, "You know, this never would've happened if you hadn't wanted to stay home to work on your trial."

"Excuse me?"

"If we'd been with Eve, this wouldn't have happened."

"Don't be stupid, Dan. This could've happened any day of any week since she reached puberty. Do you suggest we lock her up? And even if you're right, what the hell difference does it make? It did happen."

"Yeah. I know. It's just so frustrating."

"What is?"

"That we gave our all to raise her right. And then the first time she's really on her own, she sleeps with some guy whose last name she doesn't even know."

It's funny. Dad's complaint sounded perfectly reasonable. It was true--I had. I'd been so busy living in the moment that I never even thought to ask Adam his last name. But I still knew I'd done the right thing for me. I also knew there was no way in the world I'd ever be able to convince my parents of it.

"What's done is done, Dan. The question is, what are we going to do about it?"

"You really want her to have the baby?"

"Of course. As far as I'm concerned, she's already having it."

"Well, what in the world is Eve going to do with a baby? She still has a year and a half of high school. And I'm not prepared to give up my life's work to stay home with it. And you shouldn't be either, Jennifer."

"I wasn't planning to." She paused for a few moments. "Here's what I'm thinking. We're blessed. We can afford to hire a nanny for the baby and just have it be part of our family."

"Whose family?"

"Ours. Yours, mine, and Eve's."

"That's crazy. Wait. Are you suggesting we adopt it?"

"Not necessarily. Just be there for Eve and the baby."

"For the rest of its life?"

"Well, why not, Dan?"

"Because we're fucking fifty-six years old, and that's the stupidest idea I've ever heard."

Dad doesn't usually swear. Or maybe they both swear—just not in front of me. Anyway, he sounded furious. I imagined he was turning red, which I've seen him do with car salesmen. I was pretty upset about her suggestion, myself, since I have zero desire to live with my parents for the next eighteen years. Actually, for no more than the next year and a half.

"Well, I'm sure your analytical skills are better than that. Please break down that 'stupidest idea ever' point."

"I'm not breaking anything down, Jennifer. Let's just face the fact. Eve can read all the books in the world. You'll still favor her having this baby, and I'll still believe we're all insane if she doesn't have an abortion. How the hell are we going to get through this?"

"We'll just have to."

"Look, Jennifer, I know you're expecting to wear me down--that I'll eventually just give in. I know I always have. I'm a pretty flexible guy on most things. But not on this. My feelings are every bit as strong as yours, and so is my resolve." He was quiet for a minute. Then he added, "I don't think I ever told you about this, but I had a friend in medical school who got pregnant. She was single, putting herself through like you and I did, and just brimming with potential. She decided to have an abortion. There were no complications. So, she finished school and is now a pediatric oncologist at Children's. She and her husband have three great kids. Jennifer, there's no way she'd be living this life if she hadn't had the abortion."

"Who are you talking about?"

"Veronica Wiley-Davis. I don't think you've run into her. I haven't seen her at any of the benefits."

"And she just happened to tell you about her abortion?"

"I told you. She was a good friend."

"No, you didn't. You said she was a friend. So, which is it, Dan?"

"Jesus, Jennifer. What difference does it make?"

"I was just wondering why you've never mentioned this good friend before."

"Why would I? I had lots of friends before we met that I don't keep up with now."

Crap. Dad had already contradicted himself. If he hadn't kept up with Veronica, how'd he know her kids were "great"?

He went on, "I'm only telling you because she was like Eve, young and full of promise."

"Except she wasn't like Eve at all."

"What?"

"You just said this doctor woman was on her own. Eve's not on her own. We can help with any expenses—school or baby. So, she's not at all like your good friend."

I don't usually look for drama, and I was definitely in no position to judge anybody for anything. But I did think Mom's reaction sounded a little suspicious and maybe even jealous. It was possible I was seeing a problem where there wasn't one. But, it hit me that Mom was wondering whether Dad was the one who got his good friend pregnant. I was relieved she didn't say anything else about it. Number one, I didn't want to know a single thing about my parents' sex lives; and number two, we had enough trouble dealing with my pregnancy, without dragging some other lady's ancient history abortion into it.

Dad said, "I don't want to talk about it anymore right now. It'll only make things worse. But mark my words. We're in trouble here. We're in serious trouble."

I heard the door slam. Mom was apparently alone down there. Not a peep—no crying or cursing. Just silence.

Chapter 12

It was clear to me what I'd done would destroy our family. It wasn't that having an abortion or having a baby at sixteen would necessarily destroy a family. It was the fact that my parents were two super smart adults who deeply disagreed about what I should do. So, it was on me. I had to figure out a way to save us. Either the stress or the baby was making me nauseated most every day. And I couldn't do it. I couldn't figure it out.

I'll admit suicide did pass through my mind. No abortion. No baby. But also, no more Eve. And even if I'd been willing to do it—which I wasn't—I knew it wouldn't work. The truth was, it would've made my parents even more devastated. Plus, I was wasting precious time thinking up moronic ideas.

Mom gave me her three books the next day, Sunday, and I started reading right away. On Monday, Dad came home with his three. I decided to alternate and got through all six within the two weeks. I had to stay up late reading each night, and I let my homework slide a little. Plus, I felt more exhausted than I've ever felt in my life. Mom had started me on pre-natal vitamins, just in case. I was desperate to get all the reading out of the way so I could get some sleep. I wasn't the only one not sleeping. I could hear one or the other of them walking around in the middle of the nights. I wished I could just go downstairs and hug that person. Make a cup of tea for her, if it was Mom, or make hot cocoa for him, if it was Dad. But I knew this wasn't that kind of problem.

We'd agreed not to talk about *the big decision* until I'd finished the books, but it was obvious it was killing them. I didn't have to eavesdrop. They had little battles right in front of me.

Mom said ridiculous things like, "I thought you said you'd stop at the cleaners. What possible excuse do you have?" Dad's response was equally silly. "Jennifer, even you must agree that my patient's suicidal ideation is a little bit more important than your silk blouses, blah, blah, blah." I guess a couple with only one thing to argue about, who has to wait two weeks to go at it, has to grab at straws. It was insane: whose turn it was to do the dishes, how the car was parked, and whether the orange juice should've been stirred or shaken. Seriously. Like 007's martini. It was ridiculous, but nothing had ever been less funny to me. I knew that nothing I could do would smooth over what was happening. The really horrifying thing was that neither decision would solve anything. Whatever I would decide, I'd driven a wedge between the two people I loved most in the world--- well, along with Adam. And there was nothing I could say, no decision I could make, that could undo it.

I was even crazier. I just dealt with it differently—a nerd's version of shoveling down a gallon of Ben and Jerry's. I was agitated to the point of needing to vomit pretty much constantly—except when I could distract myself from the situation. Ironically, even studying fertility, abortions and the ethics stuff worked. I just had to keep my mind busy. One day when that didn't quite do it, I memorized the Gettysburg Address and the first sections of the Constitution. Unfortunately, the one thing that couldn't keep my mind occupied was homework. So, instead of studying Latin vocabulary, I memorized the full names of the Supreme Court Justices who'd heard the *Roe* case. In other words, I was totally screwed. I'd become a manic, memorizing nut—just to avoid the horror of my life. I wished I was old enough to drink. But, duh! That was one thing I knew I couldn't do without messing up the baby. My parents were both drinking. I deliberately tried not to count how many glasses of wine they each had around dinner. But it was like that old joke about not thinking about a pink elephant. Three for Mom, four for Dad. I didn't really know if that was a reasonable amount. But I knew for sure it wasn't normal for either of them. Eating was different. None of us did anything but nibble during our fake-pleasant meals.

If destroying my family weren't enough, I also ran into a huge embarrassment at school. You'd think just two weeks of poor performance would fly under the radar. And I thought it had with most of my teachers. But, on the Friday of the second week I was reading *the six books,* my trig teacher, Ms. Griffin, asked me to stay after class. It was the last period of the day, so I didn't have the excuse I needed to run to my next class.

I moved up to the front student desk in the room and she came out from behind hers and leaned her petite body against the front of it. "So, Eve, how are you doing?"

I smiled. "Fine."

"Good. That's great. Then can you tell me why you're not paying attention in class?"

"I'm not?"

"No. You seem to be somewhere far away. It's just that I've never seen you like this. I was wondering if there's something bothering you. And if you'd like to talk about it."

Tears started filling my eyes, which made me furious at myself. I thought about denying there was any problem whatsoever in my life. But I decided those ridiculous escaped tears had already given me away, so I needed to say something.

"Thanks for noticing. I thought I was hiding it pretty well. But, apparently not. Ms. Griffin, there is something going on. But it's personal and I'd rather not talk about it, if you don't mind."

She nodded her head and sighed barely audibly. "Listen, you don't have to tell me. I'm just making myself available if you decide you want to discuss it. But, whatever it is, you'll need to figure out a way to put it out of mind during class. You're one of my best students. You have real potential, Eve. I don't want to lose you to this…issue."

"Thank you. I'm sorry I was zoning out so much. I'm glad you told me. I'll do better next week."

"Well, I'm not criticizing. I just want to help."

"I know. Thanks so much."

I rose and grabbed my backpack to leave. She said, "Have a nice weekend."

"You too, Ms. Griffin!"

Crap. I really didn't like being found out. Of course, she didn't know I was pregnant. But hiding something this major was starting to make me paranoid others could tell. Well, one way or the other, my fate would be decided on the weekend. Whether I would have an abortion or start showing in another couple of months, I was likely to be distracted in class for some time.

***

Mom told me years ago that when she's training young lawyers, she always tells them to find their very best argument, and then think of the very best counter-argument. Even if it's one the opponent hasn't thought of. Because the judge may think of it. And if she doesn't, the appellate court may. Then, find your opponent's very best argument—even if he hasn't thought of it. Do the same thing. Figure out how to counter it. The rest is easy.

So, I did that with the pro-life vs. pro-choice debate. I read all the arguments, and I think the very best pro-life argument is Don Marquis'. His point is that we don't need to agonize over when a living being becomes a "person." The more important point is that once it's conceived, it has a future. It's already making its way through the stages of its life, like we all are. If it's not interrupted by nature causing a miscarriage or some doctor doing an abortion, the embryo will be a person too—and in a pretty short time. The best response was that the embryo has no self-consciousness. So, at that early stage, it really isn't quite a human. But a simple analogy beats the response. After all, an adult person in a temporary coma isn't aware of his future either. But both the adult and the embryo have one. Since they're both human futures, they must be of equal value.

Next, I focused on the very best argument for a woman's right to have an abortion. It seemed obvious. Having a baby she's not ready for will change her life. To me, it's not so much "her body/her choice." It's more that it's "her life/her choice." Women should get to live their lives the way they want, just like men do. Some woman may choose to carry an embryo when she'd rather not, but it shouldn't be required for women any more than it is for men. And it's not for men. The best response to this is that nature set it up this way, so we have no choice but to accept it. The problem with that is that we don't sit back and accept what nature dishes out in any other area.

After all, nature says disease can hurt us and kill us. But science and medicine fight it and have already won battles against tons of diseases—because we spent time and dollars on it.

I tried to simplify all this as I got ready to talk with my parents. I decided to give the best arguments on the two sides like this: 1. Pro-life. A human being (embryo) has an absolute right to its future, since it's already on the path, and 2. Pro-choice. A woman has a right to live her life without the life-changing birthing of a baby (whether or not she keeps it.) No man has to do it, and rights should be equal between men and women, who, by the way, contributed exactly the same number of chromosomes.

I definitely learned a lot. And I did come to a conclusion. I'm not saying I'm necessarily right. I'm just a sixteen-year-old girl. I'm not a doctor, or a lawyer, or a philosopher. But I have to say, it became crystal clear to me who was right. The pro-life side was right. And the pro-choice side was right. They're both right. Equally. I hadn't expected this, and I needed more time to make sense out of it.

That evening, I brought up a related topic after our usual Friday night dinner of pizza and salad. We were sitting around the kitchen table, Dad with his coffee, and Mom and I with our hot teas. I'd already cleared the table and served each of us a sundae in a small crystal goblet, which we always had on Friday nights when we were all together. I leaned back in my chair to try to look relaxed and confident.

I told my parents I'd finished reading everything. I asked them for two more days to do a little more research before we sat down for *the big talk*. They agreed. But only two days. It had to be decided soon. Then I added something I thought might take some of the pressure off them. I said, "I don't know how this will come out. But I do know this. If I have the baby, I'll do it on my own. As soon as I finish high school, I'll move out with the baby and make my own path." They glanced at each other in what looked like horror.

"Well, that's unnecessary, sweetie," said Mom. "Your father and I can easily help you financially, and we've already set aside your college money."

"Thanks, Mom. I know you guys can do it. What I'm saying is I don't want you to help me after I graduate, if I keep the baby."

"Why ever not?" she said.

"It's just that I've gotten myself into this situation, and I want to be the one to deal with it. If I have the abortion, it'll be a non-issue. But if I keep the baby, I'm committing myself to its care. I know everything will be harder, and it'll take me longer…maybe a lot longer…to finish college. But I know I can do it." I smiled. "I really think I can make it on my own. So, you guys won't have to worry about it." I nodded for emphasis.

"Eve," said Dad, "you have no idea how hard that would be. Work, rent, school, a sitter. It'll be overwhelming."

"Your father's right, Eve. You've never had anything like that kind of pressure. We've made sure you didn't have to worry about working, so you could focus on your studies. That's been your job. And you've been outstanding at it."

"The pocket money you've earned is great," said Dad. "It's not like you haven't had the experience of having jobs."

"I know. It's just something I'd want to do for myself if I have the baby." I smiled at both of them, though I already realized my idea had been stupid. This was clearly not taking any pressure off them.

"But, Eve," said Mom, "you'd be struggling when you and the baby don't need to struggle."

I made a quick decision to stick with my pitch, because I couldn't think of an alternative. "You're right, Mom. You're both right. But the thing is, I think struggle would be a good thing for me."

"Why?" asked Dad.

"I want the challenge of it." Dad shook his head like I was a foolish child. "Seriously, Dad. You and Mom both grew up poor. You put yourselves through school working minimum wage jobs. You worked your butts off to pay rent and tuition. And you made every minute count so you could study enough to keep your scholarships and do great in school. I've always envied that. I've never struggled!"

"So, you're saying we did too much for you?" said Dad.

I hesitated since I really didn't want to hurt their feelings. "Yes. But not on purpose. And most people would say I'm nuts…and ungrateful. But it's not that I don't really appreciate everything. It's just that I crave the challenge." I paused to remember how I'd practiced making my point. "I know the struggle will come in time, even if I have the abortion and go on with school as if nothing had happened. Eventually, I'll be out on my own, facing rent payments, and car payments, and limited vacation days, and all the rest of it. But if I have the baby, I'll just jump into those waters four years earlier, with a baby in my arms."

"So," said Dad, "we shouldn't use the prediction that you'll struggle as an argument against your having the baby?"

"Exactly." Having expressed my moronic idea, I pretended to relax and smiled again.

Later that night, Mom knocked on my door and came in when I said, "Yes?" I was sitting at my desk, trying to do some homework. She sat down on the corner of my bed, across from me. I swiveled my chair to look at her.

"Hi, sweetie."

"Hi. What's up, Mom?"

"I was just wondering if you wanted to talk about the boy?"

I smiled. "Adam, Mom. His name's Adam" I paused. "Sure I do. I'm glad you asked. He's really important to me, ya know?"

"I'm sorry, Eve. I should've asked you about him two weeks ago. I've just been so caught up in the pregnancy side of this."

"It's okay. I understand."

"Thanks. So, tell me all about him—Adam."

I sighed. Then a smile crept across my face. "He's the most wonderful person. So kind and gentle, and incredibly good with the little boys. He's German, actually."

"Really? So he'll be going back to Germany soon?"

"He goes back home to start college in mid-August. He loves science, like I do. And he wants to be a doctor—something I've also decided to try to do."

"Wow. Good for you, sweetie. I didn't know you'd decided."

"I guess my grades will decide for me. But, yeah, that's what I want."

"Does Adam have any siblings?"

"Hm-hm. Four younger brothers, and the littlest one is

just five! He said that's why he got along with the orphans so well. Oh, and his folks are both teachers."

"Did you two get together right away?"

"We worked together every day with the boys. I just admired him more every single day. I didn't really know if he liked me—as more than a friend—until my last night. Then I found out he felt the same way. He's hard to explain, Mom. He's just the most amazing boy I've ever met. I adore him."

Mom smiled. "So, you fell in love."

"Yeah. I really did. I can't believe it happened to me."

"That's wonderful, Eve. There's nothing in the world like the first time."

"The first time could also be the last time. I can't imagine ever getting that lucky again."

"But you will."

"Maybe. But I don't think I'll ever stop being in love with Adam. And I'm not sure I really could fall in love again. Since he's the one."

Mom bit her lip, then said, "It hurts, doesn't it?"

"What?"

"That he's not here with you."

"Yeah. It's pretty horrible." I started to tear up. Mom came over and hugged me.

"I wish I could give you advice on how to deal with that. I really don't know what to say. But, you're smart and kind, and you'll figure it out. Just remember you can talk to me about him any time. Sometimes it helps just to talk." She paused for a while, like she wanted to say something more, but wasn't quite sure. The she said, "I don't blame him, you know. If you love him, I know he must be wonderful." I just nodded.

She looked at my trig textbook, open on my desk. "I'll let you get back to it." As she opened the door to leave, she added, "I love you, Eve."

I kept my eyes on her as she walked out. "Me too, Mom."

Chapter 13

I'd planned to use my two-day reprieve from *the big decision* to study the issue some more. I put away my homework and got out all my notes on the pros and cons of abortion so I could re-read them. After an hour or so, I got the feeling I was missing something important. It kept nagging at me, but I couldn't quite put my finger on it. I was too exhausted to worry about it. It was Friday night and I didn't have to finish my homework or make a decision about the baby until Sunday evening. So, I showered and went to bed early. I was asleep the moment my head hit the pillow, and I didn't wake up until morning. But, just before I woke, an image jumped out at me. It was embryo-me in a Petrie dish, and I had a tiny arm which was pointing towards a freezer. Just a normal white enamel freezer, the kind with the top that lifts up. I said out loud, "Mom's eggs!" I was remembering what Mom had told me about how, if she'd produced any more eggs, she could've frozen them and tried again in a year or two for a brother or sister for me. Of course! That was the answer. Maybe. If science was where I needed it to be.

I looked at my clock and saw it was only 4:00 a.m. Thrilled that I had more time for research, I quickly dressed, ran downstairs for some juice and dry toast and back up to my room. I spent that day and Sunday until mid-afternoon on my computer. What I found shocked me. My idea was possible. It's called cryogenics. It's the preservation of an organism at super low temperatures so it can be revived later. And an embryo can be removed and frozen, even after it implants in the uterus. So, it isn't killed. It's just saved for later. Unfortunately, only a couple of already-attached embryos had been done, and I couldn't tell if they'd ever been thawed out and implanted in a uterus again. So, I didn't think they knew for sure it would work. But it had worked out great for mice. The embryos were removed, frozen, and then re-inserted later into a mom mouse's womb. Those mice embryos went on to become healthy baby mice. Amazing.

Of course, I'd heard of cryonics. But I always thought of it as pure science fiction. I'd read some rich dudes had themselves or loved ones frozen so they could be thawed out after the cures for their diseases had been discovered. Somehow, it just had a creepy, snake oil salesman feel about it. I kinda assumed the places that do it must all be in California.

But now I saw that cryonics and cryogenics are two different things. The removal and storage of embryos is more like IVF egg-freezing, and it's called cryogenics. It's worked beautifully for ages. Over ten thousand babies have been born this way. The mom's eggs were removed, fertilized, and frozen. This was followed, months or even years later, by defrosting and implantation. I was surprised that pregnancy rates are actually higher using frozen embryos than fresh ones. And there haven't been any birth defects or developmental problems. So far, embryos stored for up to twenty-five years have done fine.

The big difference between what's being done already, and what I was hoping to do, was that those thousands of successful procedures used embryos which hadn't gotten to the woman's uterus yet to implant. They'd been fertilized in a Petrie dish, not in a woman. They were usually from 2 to 7 days old when they got frozen. Then they got defrosted when she was ready to start being pregnant.

But, an embryo that was already attached to a uterus

would be harder. The doctor would have to remove it for freezing without hurting it or the woman's parts. The first article I found on it, from five years ago, said it is totally possible—theoretically. First, it could be done by the reverse of the "embryo transfer procedure" which has always been used to transfer IVF embryos into the mom's uterus. I read up on the embryo transfer thing and confirmed it's the exact same thing Mom did with me. Basically, embryo-me had been squirted into her uterus. So the thought was, an embryo could probably be retrieved from a woman's uterus the same way—but in reverse. I did kinda assume for the catheter tube to be big enough for my older, larger embryo, my cervix might have to be dilated, like in an abortion. A big negative.

The second way it could be done is by a laparotomy—like a C-section-- where a cut is made through the walls of my abdomen and uterus. Obviously, this would be way easier on my cervix, which wouldn't have to be dilated. And way easier on the embryo, since it would be in view and easy to reach, once the doctor gets in there. There's no chance my cervix would be hurt, and hardly any chance my uterus would be. I looked at C-sections to figure out what it would feel like. First of all, it's fairly major surgery. The cut would be horizontal, along my bikini line, maybe four to six inches long. Recovery would be about six weeks. Hardly any physical activity for the first two weeks; and nothing strenuous like soccer for two or three months--which completely sucks. Plus, it would be done under general anesthesia, so I could get gorked from that, like the brain-damaged people in the cases my mom defended. I figured it would be worth the risk to get to be asleep during all the cutting and sewing. It would also be possible my later pregnancies would have to be delivered by C-section—kind of a bummer. But, it said that's not always the case.

I was so hungry for a solution for my family that I mentally jumped at this idea--all the way to the cutting-me-open approach. I just figured if this was possible for me, I'd want to give my embryo its best chance. But the big question was whether I could find a doctor willing to do it for me. The only article I'd found on it by someone who'd actually done one was by a woman doctor in Toronto. It was from two years ago. I knew why there weren't many articles on it. One of the books I'd read explained that abortion research is really poorly funded. And at most of the medical schools that teach it, it's an elective, which means few students will take the time from their required work for it. Also, since it's a political hot potato, most researchers don't want their names anywhere near it. Even the idea of cryopreservation is taboo to some people because it's another way for a woman to end her pregnancy. Apparently, some pro-life people think carrying and raising the baby are the woman's only moral choices. But it's hard for me to believe they'd really thought that through.

The most recent article, by the Toronto fertility specialist Dr. Mary Hughey was about the two cryopreservations she'd done, after removing the embryos using a technique that sounded just like the "reverse embryo transfer." One of the women was at week 4 of her pregnancy, and the other at week 5. She said both had been successful, and the embryos looked great. They were immediately measured, photographed, and put in the preservation canisters. The women had no problems other than cramping. The doctor called the procedure "Retrieval and Preservation," which I thought was a great name. I might've gone for "Rescue and Saving for Later," but her title was probably better because it was shorter. The two embryos were still frozen when her article was published, and I couldn't find any follow-up articles. So, I assumed those two were still frozen. Nothing in the doctor's article talked about any procedure for later term pregnancies, like mine, or the possibility of a laparotomy to get to the embryo. But I did get the feeling from some of her comments that Dr. Hughey wouldn't want to do a retrieval using a catheter after 5 weeks or so. Anyway, I preferred the laparotomy, since it would give my embryo the best chance.

Honestly, I didn't have time to worry too much about the pros and cons of saving the baby this way. I was sure the good arguments on both sides could make a year-long medical ethics course, which, by the way, I'd be interested in taking… someday. Right then, however, I had only one focus: finding out if she'd do mine.

I googled Dr. Hughey. It said she was still in Toronto, and still head of a fertility clinic there. Being completely out of time to do anything but act, I sent her an email. I explained my situation, everything I could think of she'd need to know about me, and added I was ready to do it now, if it was possible for her to take me on. I pushed "send." This response came within the hour:

Dear Ms. Gehraghty,
Thank you for your letter. I cannot discuss this with you without the participation of both of your parents. If

you decide to contact me together, please call my mobile number, below, day or night. Best of luck to you.
Sincerely yours, Dr. Mary Hughey

Close enough. I was supposed to tell my parents what I wanted to do at dinner, in an hour. I was making a note card with all the points I didn't want to forget when I heard the family room door close loudly. I said, "Oh, shit," knowing it would be another argument they didn't want me to hear. At that point, I felt it was a little late to tell them I'd overheard their last two. I hadn't been expecting another one before revealing *my big decision* at 6 p.m. Feeling guilty about my eavesdropping, I'd planned to just go to the bathroom for a long bath if they ever started up again. But I needed to be ready for the dinner conversation, so I rationalized staying put and quietly listening. I sat on my floor and didn't move a muscle. It turned out I didn't need to be super-quiet. They were both speaking loudly enough for me to hear every word.

"Why do we need to talk about this before she even tells us her thoughts?"

"Because, Dan, Eve's thoughts are just her thoughts. Yes, it's important that she's looked at this thing from all angles. Of course, I'm curious to hear her take on it. But, ultimately, you and I will decide what she'll do."

"Do you care at all what Eve wants?"

Mom was quiet for a minute. "Look, Eve's already told us she doesn't know what to do. For Christ's sake, she's sixteen! We need to give her some guidance."

"Well, that would be just fine if we agreed. But how do we guide her when we're tugging two different directions?"

"You're the psychiatrist. Has it occurred to you that we go to a family therapist and get some help with this?"

"If there were any possible compromise, that might work. But our positions aren't reconcilable."

"So, we just give up?"

"I don't know, Jennifer. I don't have a solution." He paused. "Except on her idea that if she has the baby, she wants to raise it completely on her own."

"I know. I think we just humor her on that for now. If this thing moves in that direction, she'll see soon enough how foolish that would be."

"Well, I agree with that. Even if she craves 'struggling' for herself, I'm sure she won't want to deny her baby the best she could give it."

Strangely, it felt good to hear my folks agree about something, even though it was embarrassing they thought I'd made a super naïve suggestion.

"But on the main issue, Jennifer, I have no solution to our stalemate."

"Well, if we just keep delaying and discussing this to death we'll get to her twenty-fourth week and the decision will be made for us."

"Right. And you'll have won."

Mom spoke more quietly. "I'm saying I don't want the decision to be made that way. I want us to decide this together."

Dad also lowered his voice a little. "Of course. I do, too. The problem is that I think we should take her to get an abortion and you want to be a grandmother."

I thought Dad had put it badly--like this was all about Mom's craving. Mom didn't appreciate the comment either.

"Dan, you're an asshole. This isn't about me. I'd advise any young woman the same way."

"So, you're intractable?"

"Yes. Are you?"

"Yeah. I am. I'd give anything, and give up anything, to make this right for Eve."

"What does that mean?"

"I've been thinking about it. As her father, I just feel responsible to do the right thing. And it's clear to me that this problem should simply be eliminated. Tomorrow, if possible. Then we can all go back to our regular lives. The nightmare will be over."

"Like it was for that good friend of yours?"

Now I knew Mom hadn't really let that go.

"Yes. Exactly."

I thought Dad was smart not to act defensive and get sucked back into that discussion. Then, all of a sudden, Mom's voice changed. She sounded really passionate, almost pleading, when she went on. "But it can't work that way. If I gave in, and we convinced Eve to have the abortion, all the problems don't magically disappear. There could be medical issues, now or later. Issues that could make it harder for her to conceive, or to carry a baby. She could become depressed. Self-loathing. Maybe full-fledged PTSD. Also, I'd never forgive myself for agreeing to end this life. And I'd probably never forgive you. It's a nice dream, Dan, but it's not realistic."

"Well, how do you think I'll feel if I'm the one to give in? If we decide to counsel Eve to have the baby. I agree with what she said, that she wouldn't be able to give it up. It will limit her future forever. It will change her life from one brimming with promise to an indentured one. Her prospects for success in every single realm will be drastically reduced. And every day, every year that goes by, I'll know we made her do it. We refused her an early release from the problem. Yes, she may have some regret if she has the abortion. But she'll be so busy leading her life, her incredibly productive life that, my bet is, she won't dwell on it."

"So, that's it? Each one of us thinks the other's approach will basically ruin Eve's life?" said Mom, sounding exasperated.

"That's about the size of it."

It was quiet for a couple of minutes. Then Mom said, "Then I guess I'll have to raise the stakes a little, Dan--to persuade you." I had no idea where she was headed with this, and it scared the pee out of me. I actually held my breath.

"What do you mean?"

"Just this. If you don't agree.... Well, I'm thinking I'll have to leave you if you won't agree."

"What?"

"You heard me. It's that important to me. If we can't agree to support Eve in giving this human being a life…well, you'll lose all of us. Jesus, this is the only leverage I have, Dan."

There was a moment of silence downstairs. I was trying to get my head around what Mom had said. Then I heard glass break. "Jennifer, you're crazy," said Dad.

"Well, you should know. You're the psychiatrist."

"How dare you try to hold me hostage like that! Do you realize how crazy that sounds?"

"I don't know how it sounds. But I'd rather sacrifice my life than deny this child his or hers."

"You've become a pro-life nut. You're more into your

platitudes than your own family's well-being."

"Damn it, Dan! This baby *is* part of our family. And I didn't come to this ultimatum easily. I've been sick for the last week thinking about whether I could go ahead with it. I know you may not agree anyway. That I'll lose everything. Don't you see I'm only saying this out of love for you, and Eve, and yes, our grandchild. Until Eve told us she's pregnant, I didn't give a damn about grandchildren. I didn't care if Eve chose to have kids or not. We almost missed our own chance to be parents. And we would've been fine. But Eve's story is different. And I have to be true to my convictions—whatever the price."

"Jesus."

"I love you, Dan. But I can't betray my conscience. So, what do you say?"

"I can't talk about this anymore right now. I need a drink." The door slammed. This was worse than I'd thought. I'd known I was destroying my family, but until tonight, it seemed remote—something I might've magnified in my mind. Now it was actually happening. I slipped out of my room and into the bathroom. I put on the exhaust fan so they wouldn't hear me. I cried hard for a while. Sobs that came from deep inside and made my stomach heave uncontrollably. My face was so contorted I didn't even look like myself when I glanced at the medicine cabinet mirror. And then more dry heaves. I eventually stopped crying and just breathed heavily for a few minutes. I pulled myself together and decided not to be such a wimp. Somebody had to bring us back together again. And it was time for me to show some leadership out of the swamp I'd led us into.

I took a quick shower, dried my hair a little and put it in

a ponytail. Once my eyes calmed down, I got most of the red out with eye drops. I put on some mascara and a little blush. I changed into my best jeans and a cobalt blue silk top. I was going into battle, and I wanted to be dressed to take charge and fix this mess. I felt ready to make my pitch. I had to be. But I wasn't at all sure they'd agree to it.

Chapter 14

I went downstairs and peeked into the family room. Whatever glass was broken had been cleaned up. I asked Mom if it would be okay for me to make an appetizer so we could talk before sitting down to dinner. She said that was a good idea, and the slow-cooker stew could wait. I put on one of her aprons to protect my blouse and grabbed carrots, celery, and grape tomatoes from the fridge. I scooped some hummus out of its plastic container, into a small crystal bowl, and arranged the veggies around it. I took the bowl to the coffee table in the family room with paper napkins and three coasters. I offered Mom a sparkling water, but she preferred wine and got her own drink. Dad came back down the stairs and he and I both chose ginger ale, which I poured into Mom's tall, slender beer glasses. I pulled off the apron, smiled at them, and nodded toward the family room.

They sat together on the cream-colored leather couch and I sat across the coffee table from them on the edge of the overstuffed chair. I didn't want to look smaller by sinking into it. No one touched the appetizer. Mom said, "So, did you get through everything?"

"Hm-hm." I smiled again and they glanced at each other.

"So," said Dad, "what do you think?"

This was my cue. "Let me start by saying that I read all the books and I really appreciate you two digging them up for me."

"Sure," said Dad, sounding a little suspicious of my cheerfulness.

I smiled at them. "It wasn't easy to do in two weeks. But I did it. Feel free to quiz me on anything." I rattled off some random facts so they'd know I'd studied. "The egg implants in the uterus six to twelve days after it's fertilized. The embryo is the size of an orange seed at week 5, a large raspberry at week 8, and a prune at week 10. Most abortions are done in the first trimester, after which each passing week makes the procedure more dangerous. There are good arguments for and against abortion…which I'll talk about in a minute. I pulled up the *Roe vs. Wade* decision too, since so many of the articles I read talked about it, and I like to see for myself what's what. Like I thought, it confirmed abortions in the first trimester are legal. But I'd had no idea it was for a practical reason-- more women actually die in childbirth than by having an abortion in the first three months. Anyway, my decision will be purely a moral one." I stopped for a moment and just looked at them. They didn't say anything, so I said, "So, do you want to quiz me?"

Mom said, "No, Eve. I believe you studied the material."

"Yeah. Absolutely," said Dad.

"Good. Because the way I see it, we need to make a decision tonight. And there is literally not enough time in one night to go over all the thoughtful analysis that smart people on both sides of the debate have done."

"Agreed," said Mom. Dad nodded. They both looked nervous as hell, but now that I'd started talking, I wasn't the least bit shaky.

"Then let me get to the bottom line." I paused for effect. "I think the pro-life argument is right."

Mom gasped and said, "Thank God!" She started to get up to hug me, but I stood and said, "I wasn't finished, Mom."

We sat back down and she said, "Oh. All right."

"I also think abortion is a reasonable way for me to go under all the circumstances."

Mom said, "Why are you messing with me?"

Okay. So, I'd badly miscalculated how to be dramatic about it, and hurt her feelings. "Sorry, Mom. I said that badly. I didn't mean it as a trick. May I finish?"

"Sure," she said dismissively, as though she expected nothing more helpful to come out of my mouth.

"What I've learned over the past two weeks is that you are both the most principled people I know. Mom, believing abortion is the killing of a human being—well, you couldn't live with yourself if you didn't do everything you could to save the baby. And, Dad, since you're convinced I have a right, really a duty, to guard my own life and focus on the good things I can do in the future, I don't think you could live with yourself if you gave in to Mom or anybody else. I think you both have to tell me your real opinions, even if it costs you." I knew I was laying it on pretty thick.

They were both staring at me intently, probably wondering where in the world I was headed. I was getting teary. "The thing is, I really appreciate your strength in standing up for your convictions. It breaks my heart I've forced you guys to confront the unconfrontable." I used the backs of my hands to wipe away the tears sliding down my cheeks. I was irritated they'd leaked out, which wasn't part of the plan. I'd wanted to be as together as possible.

I wasn't sure I was reading their expressions right, but they seemed committed to patiently waiting for me to get to my decision. I went on, "Now that I've read up on it, I'm super impressed with people in this country, on both sides of this, who are living their morality. Well, with the exception of the ones who started getting violent in '93. You know, they actually murdered doctors who did abortions."

"I know," said Mom. "But that was a tiny minority."

"Yeah. I kinda figured. So, after I thought about everything, I realized both sides are right. Equally. I'd really like to explain why."

Mom said, "Sure. That's why we're here." But she looked mystified.

Dad added, "We're all ears, Eve."

I took a moment to take a couple of sips of my drink. "On the pro-life side, I was convinced by the argument that an embryo has a right to its future, since it's already on its path through life—just like we all are. It doesn't matter that it isn't aware of its future. A child in a temporary coma isn't aware of his either. But they both have them—human futures--so how can they not be of equal value?" Mom nodded, but Dad just sat there listening.

"On the pro-choice side, women should have exactly the same right as men to live their lives as they want. Men don't have to carry unwanted embryos, so women shouldn't have to either. And it shouldn't matter that nature set it up that way, since we spend fortunes to fight what nature sets up in every other area." Now Dad was nodding, and Mom was just sitting there listening. "Guys, I've realized the people on both sides of the debate are so passionate because they really think they're right. Because they really are right. See, they're both right." I smiled since I was proud of having figured it out. Since they didn't smile back, I knew none of what I'd said actually gave them a clue about what I wanted to do. "Before I go on, I'd just like to say something obvious that's really interesting to me. The best way out of this is Claire's idea of really good birth control from puberty—like for every girl in the world." They looked at me like they didn't appreciate my getting off track. "Sorry. So, now I want to tell you what I've figured out for me. I just want you to hear me out first. Then we can discuss the details over dinner. Okay?"

They both nodded, then let out deep breaths, which I took as, "Finally!".

"Mom, you told me all about how I was conceived in vitro." I smiled at her.

"It feels like a hundred years ago."

"Well, yesterday I was worrying this thing to death and remembered that you'd told me that if you'd had extra eggs, they could've been fertilized with Dad's sperm and frozen to be used later." I'm not sure, but it looked like Dad was a little embarrassed at me talking about his sperm. But I'd chosen it over semen so he'd be less uncomfortable. Anyway, Mom was now smiling, so I dove in.

"I'd always thought of human cryonics as sci-fi nonsense. And, basically, it still is for adults and children. Well, for any fully-formed person who isn't still inside a uterus. Although there may be a future in it down the line." They were both staring at me really intently. "Well, the thing I didn't realize is that cryopreservation of embryos isn't at all like cryonics. It's much closer to an IVF done with a frozen embryo, rather than a fresh one."

"I hadn't thought about that. You may be right," said Mom, almost to herself.

"There are literally millions of test tube people walking around who were conceived like I was, and then implanted. And there are over ten thousand people who were frozen as embryos and later transferred into the mom's uterus. No birth defects or problems have ever been found in any of those babies."

"But, Eve, your embryo has already implanted," said Dad.

"Of course. That was around January 18th. But, what's new in medicine today, what I had no idea about, is post-implantation cryogenic freezing of an embryo."

"Has this been done?" asked Mom.

"Yes. According to the articles I was able to find, and I'm sure there's more. At least two first-trimester embryos have been surgically removed and cryogenically frozen so they can be implanted at a later time, when the woman wants to get pregnant."

"How did they work out?" said Mom.

"They don't know yet. They're still frozen, as far as I can tell."

"Oh," said Dad.

"But, this whole process has worked really well for lab mice and the mice babies were perfect."

"How do they remove the embryo from the womb?" asked Mom.

"The way I understand it, the doctor used the reverse of the 'embryo transfer procedure' that put embryo-me into your uterus."

"Really?" said Dad. "So, how is that done exactly?"

"The doctor had to dilate the woman's cervix, like for an abortion. Just so there'd be enough room to get the 4 or 5-week embryo out. Of course, she needed a larger removal tube than the one that was used to insert me."

Dad said, "She just sucked them out?"

"Yeah. Basically."

Mom asked, "When were those two done?"

"The article I found was from two years ago. There were a number of other more general articles, but only the one about the actual procedure having been done. Apparently, there are lots of reasons why research isn't well-funded for this, and why findings aren't written up."

"I can imagine," said Dad.

"Right. But this doctor, Mary Hughey from Toronto, described what she'd done in detail."

"So, Eve, is that what you want to try to do?"

"Yeah, Mom. I really do. But I have a feeling she couldn't do mine with the tube thing... since I'm already at 8 weeks."

"You think your embryo is too large?" said Dad.

"Yeah. I'm pretty sure it is. But that's actually fine with me, since I'm more interested in having a laparotomy."

"Really?" said Mom.

"I read in an earlier article that it really should work well. See, if the doctor opens me up, she'd be able to see the embryo better, which would be safer for it. And less chance that anything wrong would happen to my uterus. Plus, no risk at all to my cervix."

"Yes. But a laparatomy adds the risks of major surgery," said Mom.

I answered slowly and calmly, so she'd know that fact didn't bother me. "I know. That's true, Mom. And I'm okay with it." I smiled at her. She didn't really smile back, so I didn't know what she was thinking.

"Do you think this Dr. Hughey is reputable?" Dad asked.

"I do. But I happen to have two parents who know exactly how to find out." Mom and Dad both chuckled, which was a relief.

Dad got serious again right away. "Do you know if she's still doing this?"

"I think so. I emailed her yesterday and she got back to me right away."

"That's interesting. What did she say, Eve?" asked Mom.

"She was very polite. But, basically, she said she couldn't talk to me without both of my parents."

Mom said, "That's a good sign."

"Oh, and she gave me her cell number."

Mom said, "This is all very interesting, sweetie. But let's not get our hopes up."

Dad added, "You really want to pursue this. Right?"

"Yeah. Very much, Dad."

Mom said, "What do you think, Dan?"

"I think we need to be cautious. But there's no harm in looking into it. And time is critical." He looked at Mom. "Are you okay with this?"

"Yes. Let's talk with this Dr. Hughey."

"Good. Eve, get me that cell number and I'll call her right now. And your mother and I will use our resources to check her out from our offices in the morning. If she's willing, I'll try to get us an appointment with her for Tuesday. We can always cancel if her credentials don't pan out. It's a long-shot she'll see us right away. Are you clear Tuesday, Jennifer?"

"I'll make sure I am."

"Eve, you'd have to miss a day of school."

"No problem. No tests scheduled for Tuesday."

I ran up to my room to jot down the phone number,

my heart racing. Glancing in my mirror, I realized I had a big grin on my face. When I got back downstairs, Dad rang the number, and after a few moments, he was speaking with Dr. Hughey. They talked about general background stuff for a while and Dad confirmed what I'd said in my e-mail. He told us afterward that the doctor said this was a good time for her and that she'd be happy to meet with the three of us on Tuesday at 3:00 at her clinic, but that if everything was a go, she'd wait no longer than Friday to do the procedure, since every day that goes by makes it more dangerous for me. That word "dangerous" sucked a little of the excitement out of me, so I tried to forget she'd said it.

By the time we walked into the kitchen and set out everything for our dinner, my parents seemed more relaxed than they'd been since I'd delivered my news fifteen days earlier. Almost like they were when we were happy. I could feel them trying to act more subdued than they felt.

We discussed the procedure as something that might be widely available to women in the future, and imagined lots of benefits. Mom said, "This could be the solution for women, or couples, who get pregnant before they're ready and then find out they're not terribly fertile once they're older and ready to try for a baby."

Dad added, "There would be so many options for that frozen embryo, even when the couple decides not to have it implanted in the original mom. Donation to infertile couples…."

I interrupted, still wanting to show off my knowledge. "Exactly. Twelve percent of American couples have infertility problems, Dad. That's a lot of people."

"It sure is." He continued, "Gay couples and maybe infertile relatives of the donor couple, who would really like to have some of the family genes in their child."

I wanted to focus more on girls like me. "It would be a huge relief for a young woman who wants children but isn't remotely situated to do her best for them. Especially if she can't quite stomach the idea of killing it."

That kinda yanked Dad back into the original discussion. He said, "So, if this doesn't pan out with Dr. Hughey, are you saying you're one of those people?"

"Not necessarily. I'm convinced that a living being, having the full 46 chromosomes to make it a human, has the right to keep progressing—like we all do. I mean, we're all just at different stages of our passage through life. What the embryo already owns is its future—which it'll have unless somebody steps in to kill it. That's what I find convincing."

"I see."

"But, I also think that a woman has the right to live her life without being made to carry an unwanted baby. Why should she have to, when half the chromosomes came from the guy?"

Mom answered, "Well, like you said earlier, it is how nature works."

"I know. As in, 'tough luck, women!'"

"Basically."

"Well, Mom, we shouldn't accept that. In no other area of medicine or science do we just say, 'Tough luck! Nature just made it that way! Damn bad luck for you women!'" I looked at each of them to slow myself down. I know I talk too fast when I get excited about an idea. "I've been thinking about artificial limbs for people born without them or who got separated from theirs in some stupid war. What about the separation of conjoined twins or repair of a cleft pallet? Heck, breast implants and nose jobs—they're all changing what nature dealt us. And nobody complains about those, do they? Nobody says medicine shouldn't interfere because 'that's just how nature works.' Why shouldn't science and medicine level things out for women?"

"Eve, I see you've given all of this a lot of thought," said Dad, who'd only taken one bite of his stew.

"Not nearly enough, Dad. Twelve days, during school weeks, didn't give me remotely enough time to really analyze it. I feel like I'm just starting to scratch the surface. But can't you guys see the truth in each other's arguments?"

"Yes," said Mom. "I think we all do get entrenched. And once we do, we become almost incapable of seeing the truth in the other side's position. You are a very fair-minded person, sweetie. I'd like to be more like that." She was also ignoring her meal. I felt like the food was a minor distraction, so I also ignored it.

"Me too," said Dad. "When I focus on only what I believe, I just keep reinforcing my correctness. Because, as you point out, my pro-choice view *is* correct. What neither your mother nor I has done is to really look at the other side's reasoning. I hate to admit this, Eve, but you may be right. Both positions may be correct, depending on which one we're focusing on."

"That's exactly it, Dad. It's all about focus. It's like when you go outside on a beautiful starlit night. You look up to see the Big Dipper. Or is it Big Bear? They're both there. You just adjust your vision so you notice one more than the other. They're both true at the same time. But I may see the Big Dipper, while you're seeing Big Bear."

"What a lovely analogy, Eve," said Mom.

"It's just something I've been thinking about. So, in answer to your question, Dad, my only decision is to try to work with Dr. Hughey."

Dad said, "I'm really proud of you. And whatever happens, I'll still be proud of you."

"As will I, sweetie," said Mom.

As I got ready for bed that night, I felt almost serene for the first time since I did the pee test. All the tension had lifted from our house, just the way a fog does. But I also knew we were all three borderline crazy to be putting so much stock in what Dr. Hughey might be able to do to save us. What if she found I wasn't a good candidate for some reason? Or, what if her credentials didn't pan out? Maybe my parents would learn tomorrow morning that she was as delusional as we were. Or maybe she's a brilliant doctor, but when she explains the risk, we just can't do it? I finally decided to try to stop worrying about it. We'd all find out what was possible in two days.

Chapter 15

On Monday morning, I put my phone on silent and snuck it into school in my bra. I went to the restroom after each class to see if Mom or Dad had texted me about Dr. Hughey's reputation. Nothing came through until my lunch break at 11:30. It was from Mom:

Hughey: Well-respected. Innovative. Excellent results at her fertility clinic. Only general information about freezing embryo post-implant.

Sounded good to me. I was dying to think through what this would mean for me, but I had to try to concentrate on my classes that afternoon. I took this especially seriously in view of Ms. Griffin's warning, and I wondered if any of my other teachers had noticed I'd been present only in body for the past two weeks. I didn't tell Claire what was going on because I really wanted to find out first what Dr. Hughey would say—whether it was a bust or a go.

Dad had come home early from work because of our trip the next morning. When I walked in the back door, he told me what he'd found out about Dr. Hughey was also good. He gave me a thumbs-up. Then he said the words that actually made my heart flutter. "Oh, Eve, I almost forgot. A letter came for you today from the Dominican Republic. It has the orphanage's return address, so it's probably a thank-you note or something."

"Where is it?"

"I put it on your bed so you wouldn't miss it."

I said, "Great! Thanks, Dad," and ran up the stairs. I really didn't think it would be from Adam. It was more like an urgent hope. I tore it open. The letter was handwritten on yellow notebook paper. I didn't need to look at the signature to know it was from him.

Dear Eve,

I hope you are able to read my handwriting and will forgive that this may take some time to reach you. Jan kindly gave me your email address and your postal address in Chicago. As you know, we have no wi-fi here, so this is the best I can do.

I wish I had been able to formulate my thoughts and share them with you in person. But we had so little time. I want you to know how much meeting you has meant to me. From the first moment, over pancakes and plantains, I never laid eyes on you without seeing radiant warmth, kindness and openness.

I won't risk boring you by commenting on your beauty and grace. I'm sure you hear that quite often. (If not, you should.) But many women are beautiful and graceful. That is not what sets you apart. You said you thought I was gifted with the little boys, but that you were not. I think you are wrong. Please remember the day I asked you to skip the volunteer beach trip and stay back with me to care for the boys. Well, you would have been my first choice to work with me...for selfish reasons. But I did not choose. I asked the boys who they would like for me to ask to be with us for the day. They'd been with many other volunteers by that time. They answered immediately, all screaming. "Eve!" So, I asked them, "Porque?" Here are some of the answers they gave: "Eve doesn't rush me," "Eve always gets down on her knees and looks right at me when I talk," and "Eve is calm. I hate the way most of the volunteers act so excited all the time." But, my favorite answer was, "Eve loves us." To that I said, "How do you know?" And Jose said, "Es claro." (It's clear.)

Eve, you are not like any girl I have met. I wish so much we had been together for a longer time. Now, when I go to our spot to look at the heavens, I feel like you are with me. It is not so practical to think I will see you again. At least, not for a long time. I did not mention that it is my hope to win a scholarship to medical school in the United States. But that is four years away, and the United States is a big country. I do not know where I would be, or where you will be by then.

I hope we can keep in touch by text and Face Time once I return home. I am not asking you to wait for me in any way. You must meet people, and date other boys. (I am already jealous of all of them.) And I should be practical and try to be open to other girls, although I know I will compare all of them with you. And it is hard for me to imagine that they won't pale in the comparison.

I just wanted you to know that I admire you, and I crave to be with you. I miss you very much already. I will send you a text when I arrive home to ask whether you would still like to keep up our friendship. I just wanted to let you know how much you mean to me.

With all my love,
Adam

My first thought was, Oh my God! Adam really feels about me the way I feel about him. No one had ever said things like this to me before. I tried to understand how he could see all of this in me, when he was the one. He was the ideal. Mainly, his letter made me question my decision not to tell him about the baby. He was so good to me, and I wasn't sure I was being good to him.

Then it hit me that he hadn't included his phone number or his email address--no home address. Worse, I still didn't know his last name. As far as he knew, we'd simply begin talking in mid-August. By then, I'd be two months from his baby's due date. Or not.

***

We all got up early on Tuesday morning for our 7:00 a.m. flight to Toronto. Mom had booked the earliest flight so we'd have other options if ours were cancelled for some reason. We checked in at Terminal 1 and saw that our flight was, in fact, delayed. An airline employee told us that it was mechanical trouble. Mom asked him if we could simply move to a later flight that looked like it would be on schedule. She said since we didn't have any luggage she hoped this would work, and we needed to be in Toronto for a 3:00 meeting. He said he'd love to help us out, but the remaining flights that would get us to Toronto in time were overbooked. He suggested we stick with our original flight and just wait at the gate for updates. He added that mechanical issues are often resolved without much delay. Mom and Dad both flew enough to know that it was a completely meaningless statement. Even I knew it from my limited but usually disappointing experience with flying. I suggested we rent a car and drive there, but Dad told me it was an eight-hour drive, plus the time to get the car, traffic issues, and the delay to go through customs at the border. So, it turned out Mom's plan to take the earliest flight to guarantee we'd make our appointment hadn't really worked out. We had all our eggs in one basket—and the airline dropped our basket.

We had just gotten to our gate in concourse B when a man walked up to Mom, stretched out his hand, and said, "Jennifer! How are you, dear?" He was tall with dark, slicked-back hair and was wearing an expensive-looking black coat. He had a black, alligator briefcase, shined to a glow, in his other hand. The same glow was on his shoes, so it must've been like a matched set.

"Well, Joel, what are you doing in Terminal 1? Slumming?"

He smiled, clearly appreciative of Mom's comment. She turned to Dad and said, "This is my husband, Dan." They shook hands. Then she nodded toward me and said, "And this is our daughter, Eve. Dan, Eve, this is Joel Nepolitano." Joel barely glanced at Dad, but he definitely gave me the once-over.

Then he said to me, "Eve, you look just like your beautiful mother. Where are you off to, dear?"

I hated him already but knew Mom and Dad would expect me to be nice. "Thank you. We're headed to Toronto for me to visit a couple of colleges, York and Ryerson. It's so hard for Mom and Dad to get away. So I'm thrilled to have this little day trip with them."

Joel looked at Mom and said, "She's lovely, Jennifer." Then he winked at me. I felt like barfing.

"What're you up to, Joel? I thought you always took your own plane to avoid the riff-raff," said Mom.

"Actually, I'm sneaking off to Spain with my girlfriend for a couple of weeks. So, from here to La Guardia, then direct to Madrid."

"That's wonderful, Joel. You deserve a break after drafting up all of those lawsuits against my clients. You poor thing. You must be exhausted."

He was standing close to Mom and patted her on the arm. "It's certainly worth the effort, to get to see you at the depositions." This guy was a total worm. I glanced up at Dad, who had the most strained smile I'd ever seen--like it was about to explode. This guy was totally flirting with Mom, and I had the feeling Dad was about to punch him. It was so weird to watch. Here, I'd been thinking a lot about Mom's eggs and Dad's sperm. But I'd completely missed seeing that they were still sexual beings. Mom really was beautiful. Her sleek, auburn page-boy really accentuated her green eyes. And the delicate freckles over the bridge of her nose made her look younger than she was. Slender and stylish, she was apparently still very attractive to men. This made me look at Dad more objectively, too. He was more handsome than Joel, but not nearly as polished looking. Dad was also tall and slender, but balding on top, with his hair in the back just a little too long. He was wearing out-of-fashion wire-rim glasses. His trench coat was no match for Joel's cashmere—or whatever the heck it was.

I said, "Unfortunately, our flight's delayed for mechanical reasons and the later ones are all full."

Dad spoke up as though I was annoying Mr. Nepolitano. "It'll be fine, Eve." Then, turning to Mom's admirer, "It was nice meeting you, Joel, but I'm sure you want to get to your gate."

He glanced at Dad, then spoke to Mom. "Jennifer, I really don't want your charming daughter to worry about your flight. He reached inside his coat, and into the breast pocket of his suit jacket, pulled out a business card, and handed it to Mom. "You really must take my plane. It's just down the road twenty minutes at Chicago Executive—Milwaukee and Palatine Roads. I'll text my pilot, Hank. All you need to do is call him on his cell and tell him when you'll be there. By the time your cab gets you there, he'll have the plane pulled out and ready to go. Hank's great. He'll get you to Toronto in plenty of time." He pulled out his phone and sent a quick message.

I said, "Wow."

Joel looked at me and said, "I just keep him on standby. This will give the guy something to do with his day."

Mom said, "Oh, Joel. That's very kind. But we can't accept such a..."

I interrupted, "Mr. Nepolitano, I'm really hoping our flight gets cleared. But after getting Mom and Dad to make this trip with me, I would just feel terrible if we couldn't get to Toronto. If you're really sure, I thank you from the bottom of my heart." I smiled sweetly.

"Eve!" said Dad.

"No. No. It's really my pleasure." Now he patted my arm, and I feared his sliminess would leave a mark on my sleeve. Then he added, "I love a woman who knows how to accept a gift. Please call Hank." He shook hands with each of us and added, "I have to go rustle up Heather. She scooted off to buy earphones."

"It was wonderful to meet you!" I said, as he turned toward the Hammacher and Schlemmer shop. We all watched him rendezvous with Heather, a thirty-something blonde in stiletto heels. I'm sure Mom and Dad thought of it too-- she was probably a woman who knew how to accept a gift.

Dad turned to me, "What was that act all about?"

"Getting to Toronto."

Mom said, "And how did you happen to know the Toronto colleges?"

"Just being prepared, Mom."

Mom said, "Well, let's check the monitor to see how it's looking. We walked over to one of the wall displays and all saw the bad news at the same time. "7 a.m. Chicago to Toronto—CANCELLED."

"Shit," said Dad.

"Thank goodness we have a backup plan." I smiled at him, but he didn't smile back.

Dad said, "Excuse us a minute, Eve. I need to speak with your mother." They stepped about four feet away, and I could hear every word.

"Jennifer, that's one creepy guy."

"I know."

"I don't think we should accept his offer. I don't want you beholden to him."

"We need to get to Toronto, Dan. I'll just take him to lunch some time at a swanky restaurant."

"Over my dead body."

"Why, you're jealous."

"I am not. He's just such a snake."

"I know. I've had cases against him for years. How about

this? We both take Joel and Heather out to a nice dinner some evening?"

"You've got to be kidding."

"Okay. So, we send him a dozen bottles of good wine?"

"Fine. But I don't like this one bit."

"Yes, I can see that. I don't like it either, Dan. But we really do need to get to Toronto."

"All right." He kissed Mom on the cheek. "I love you."

"I know. I love you, too."

The day was already like none I'd ever seen, and we hadn't even gotten to the plane yet.

It took the cab from O'Hare about forty minutes to get us to the little airport. As we pulled up, Dad said to the driver, "Didn't this used to be called Palwaukee?"

"It sure did. I come out here a lot—just not usually from O'Hare."

"We don't normally airport hop, either," said Mom, as Dad paid the fare.

It struck me as a pretty classy place, friendly people and nice refreshments. An older man, in a leather jacket and tan slacks, walked up to us and said, "Jennifer Gehraghty's party?"

Mom smiled and shook his hand. "You must be Hank."

He turned to Dad, who introduced himself as Dan, and then to me. We all shook hands. "Are you folks ready to head to Toronto?"

"Absolutely!" I answered, thrilled to be able to make my appointment and to have a ride in a cool small plane.

"Good. My co-pilot, Leigh, is at the plane. Shall we head out?"

As we made our way to the plane, Dad had lots of questions for Hank. "What model is it?"

"Mr. Nepolitano has a beautiful Cessna Citation."

Dad just looked at Hank. "So, for how long have you worked for him?"

"Since I retired. Going on ten years."

"And you still call him Mr. Nepolitano?" asked Dad. Mom gave him a look.

"His choice."

Dad dropped it. "Is it a turbojet?"

"Exactly."

"So, will you fly in to Pearson?"

"No. We'll land at Billy Bishop."

"Where's that?"

"Just a small island airport right off the city. Less busy. And, Dan, it's right near downtown. Quicker through customs this way too."

"Great. That sounds fine, Hank. Thanks."

After all the stress at O'Hare, Hank was so friendly and confident that I began to relax. I was sure he'd get us to my appointment on time. Once we were in the air, I was struck by how similar it was to a commercial flight. Dad said he thought we were at around 39,000 feet, though I have no idea how he knew. There were clouds below us, so the view was no different than on a commercial flight. I'd been hoping for something more like the prop plane that once took us from Miami to Key West. I don't know how many feet we'd been above the ground, but I could see everything—the iridescent turquoise water and the lush keys, one after another. Coming from a deep-freeze Chicago winter, I'd thought it looked like salvation.

I eventually got so relaxed that I nodded off, and woke

up when the wheels hit the landing strip. We'd done it! It was only 1:00 and we were in Toronto. Getting through customs was a cinch. Then we had to walk through a tunnel under Lake Ontario to get to the city side where the cabs were lined up. It's funny. When I fly, I never focus on the fact I'm in a small tube, whizzing through the air at 400 mph. But I was super aware of walking through the tunnel—a pipe sitting on the bottom of an ice cold Great Lake. I'm pretty sure I held my breath until we passed through the exit and into the sunlight—like that would've done any good in the event of a leak.

Chapter 16

A cold breeze blew off the lake, but the day was gorgeous. The sky was an unusual deep color that reminded me of Mom's favorite bedspread. She calls it Williamsburg blue. Our cab pulled up to a sleek high-rise. There was no sign out front that the building had a fertility clinic, or any medical offices at all. The only clue was how near it was to a sprawling hospital complex. But it was definitely the address Dr. Hughey had given Dad. Once we'd entered the building through a revolving door, a middle-aged receptionist greeted us and asked if she could help. Dad gave her Dr. Hughey's name and she pointed to one of the two elevator banks. "Take one of the elevators, just there. She's on the twelfth floor."

"Is there a suite number?" asked Mom.

"Oh no. Dr. Hughey has the entire floor. You'll see her receptionist when you step out of the elevator."

"Thank you," said Dad.

"You're very welcome. And have a lovely day." She smiled warmly.

Once we were alone in the elevator, I mentioned how friendly the cab driver and the receptionist had been.

"Canadians are known for it," said Mom. I thought it was terribly cool for an entire country to have a reputation for warmth. I didn't think the United States was likely to be mistaken for Canada. We stepped out of the elevator and up to a glass wall separating us from Dr. Hughey's offices. According to the list stenciled on the door, Dr. Hughey had four other doctors in her practice—all women. We were greeted by a heavy-set older woman receptionist, wearing a red skirt suit and a white blouse with a bow at the neck. Dad gave her our names and told her we had a 3:00 appointment with Dr. Hughey. She smiled brightly and said that the doctor would be out promptly at that time to meet us. But, since it was only 2:00, we should help ourselves to the coffee or tea on the bureau, and Tim Horton pastries, whatever those were. Her white hair and cheerfulness brought Mrs. Claus to mind. I just hoped I'd be getting what I'd asked for, even though Santa might not think I'd been a good girl this year.

The waiting area was bright and pleasant, with a great view of downtown Toronto and Lake Ontario. The lake was shimmering—like it was winking at me. Several of the lakefront buildings really stretched themselves toward the sky, but none came close to the height of the CN Tower. I'd read it was Toronto's most famous symbol, and that its observation deck is the highest one in the world. I was jealous of all the people who'd come as tourists instead of pregnant sixteen-year-olds. I stood at the window and watched the traffic below, while Mom and Dad both opened their laptops and began to do work stuff. It had never really hit me before that professionals pretty much work constantly. Mom and Dad usually open their laptops after dinner and sit reading and typing until the 10 p.m. news. They try to take weekends off, but succeed only when they don't have big projects due the following week: important court papers or trial prep for Mom, and lectures or articles for Dad. The odd thing is that neither of them seems to be the least bit disappointed to have to spend their time like that. It's almost like work is both the way they make their livings and their favorite hobby. I certainly hope I love my work enough to want to be at it in my free time. I think.

It took hours for 3:00 to arrive, and just as Mrs. Claus had predicted, Dr. Hughey walked into the reception area at exactly that time. She was a large woman with short gray hair, and very Canadian. That is, she was very friendly. She was also as dark as the night sky, and her eyes shown like bright stars. I liked her immediately. Dr. Hughey asked about our trip as she walked us to her office. I told her that Mom's friend had loaned us his Cessna for the flight.

"Well, how did you enjoy that, Ms. Gehraghty?"

"Please, call me Eve, if it's okay with you. The flight was wonderful. I'd love to take a ride like that at night. To feel like I was as close to the stars as I could be."

"You appreciate the stars?"

"Yes. I can't get enough of constellations." My parents exchanged a look. I'd never once star-gazed with them and I'd never raved about the stars before. They must've wondered what the heck I was talking about. Then again, maybe they assumed it had something to do with the orphanage trip.

Dr. Hughey took us through her tidy office to an adjacent small conference room, where we all sat down at a round mahogany table. "Mr. and Mrs. Geraghty, Eve, I'd like to review where we are and explain what we may be able to accomplish. If you have questions along the way, please feel free to interrupt me. But before we get started, would anyone care for tea, coffee…a cola?"

"Thanks, no," said Dad.

"Not for me. Thanks," said Mom.

I said, "I could use a glass of water. I mean, if it's not too much trouble."

Dr. Hughey smiled at me. "Excellent idea, Eve." She got

up and walked to a phone on the wall and requested a pitcher of water and four glasses. I was glad she did, since I needed to sip mine frequently during the meeting. I hadn't realized how nervous I was until I noticed that my right knee was shaking under the table.

She started with my health background, then asked about when I started my periods, and finally got to my pregnancy. I told her that I could pin down the timing pretty well since I'd only had sex once. Although it was embarrassing to talk about it in front of my parents, I did appreciate that they let me talk for myself without interrupting or correcting me. I also liked that Dr. Hughey kept her eyes on me while we talked and didn't glance at Mom and Dad for confirmation. She took notes on a yellow legal pad. It was the same kind of paper as Adam's letter.

She explained what she does in general--infertility treatment--and what she'd been working on in cryopreservation of embryos, post-implantation. She said she'd always specialized in helping couples who were having trouble getting pregnant. "But about six years ago, it occurred to me that I might be able to come up with a procedure to cryopreserve embryos that had already implanted in the uterus. I never expected it would be a volume practice, even if I could get to the point where it could be done reliably using something simple, like the reverse embryo transfer." She sighed and added, "Frankly, the better way to eliminate unwanted pregnancies would be innovations in contraception, to make it more readily available for every woman. But nothing involving the human factor will ever be perfect. So safely ending a pregnancy, while also saving the embryo, seemed like an obvious solution for women who simply want their baby to come later. I call what I do Retrieval and Preservation."

"How many have you done? I mean, any since the two described in your article?" asked Dad.

"Actually, I haven't found another interested patient who was still early enough in her pregnancy for the reverse transfer to be viable. Have you all had the chance to read my article?"

Mom spoke up, "Yes, we have. After Eve did the heavy lifting by finding it. You make it very clear how the ultrasound helped you make the withdrawal at exactly the right spot."

"It would be impossible without the ultrasound."

"Well, it's very impressive," said Dad. "Since we couldn't find anything beyond your first article, we assume neither embryo has been defrosted at this point."

"That's right."

"Dr. Hughey, do you know when you might be able to defrost one?" I asked, and then added, "Aren't you dying to know if it worked?".

"I certainly am. Hopefully, it won't be too long. One of the couples were graduate students when theirs was done two and a half years ago. In fact, both the mother and the father were studying microbiology. They've told me recently it should be within the next year for them."

I said, "That's great!" and smiled. I saw that neither of my parents was really smiling. In fact, they looked pretty somber.

"Yes. It is great, Eve. As I said in the article, the embryos both looked good. But defrost and re-implantation of post-attachment embryos has never been attempted. Everything rests on the success of the embryos."

"As my husband mentioned to you on the phone, Eve's

interested in having a laparotomy. What are your thoughts on that approach for her?"

Dad interjected, "Since she's passed 9 weeks, she thinks it's too late for her to have the other procedure."

"Eve is right. Her embryo is too large for the catheter. Actually, the laparotomy will be easier on the embryo, since I'll be able to visualize everything I'm doing. Obviously, no dilation of the cervix will be needed. Just a standard laparotomy and extraction."

"Has any other woman requested the laparotomy?" asked Mom.

"No. The truth is, Mrs. Gehraghty, there are few volunteers for either procedure because abortion is so readily available and reliable. And none of the women I've met with was willing to go through the laparotomy and endure the six-week recovery time. They were past my cut-off for the transfer procedure, so laparotomy had been their only option."

"Interesting. And they all declined," said Mom.

"Yes. They weren't willing to have major surgery."

"So, what did they do?" I asked.

"I don't know, Eve. I never heard." She smiled at me.

Dad asked, "Will Eve's procedure definitely be done under a general?"

"Yes. We'll have to use a general. I'll rely on the ultrasound for best placement of the incision." She turned to me, "And, Eve, when you wake up, it'll all be over."

"Except knowing what to do with the frozen embryo," I said.

"Actually, things like that tend to work themselves out in the twenty-five years that we can preserve it for you."

"Where are the frozen embryos kept?" asked Mom.

Dr. Hughey walked to the large plate-glass window and pointed to a building about a block away. "I share the storage facility with the hospital. It's state-of-the-art and monitored 24/7 by hospital staff. There were a couple of mishaps in the states, so now there are also monitors for the monitors."

"And after the twenty-five years are up?" I asked.

"At that time, it must be implanted in the original mother, after she's been prepared to receive it. Or it can be donated or disposed of."

I didn't like hearing the words "disposed of," but twenty-five years did seem like enough time to decide on the next step. I've never been against the idea of circumstances helping make decisions. It happens all the time. I expected the answer would make itself clear to me in less than two-and-a-half decades.

"Do you have any questions, Eve?"

"What are the chances this will work out for the embryo?"

She crinkled her eyes as she thought for a moment. "Theoretically, there's no reason it shouldn't work. But, nothing's perfect in real life. I believe your embryo should have an excellent chance to do well—long term."

"Hm. Thanks, doctor."

"Mr. and Mrs. Gehraghty? Any questions?""

"No," Mom and Dad said at the same time.

"Of course, I'll need consents from your parents and you, Eve. Since you're under age."

"Consents for what?" I asked.

"Statements that I've explained the surgery to you, the risks and complications, and that you agree I should store the frozen embryo for a period of twenty-five years, or until you request it, either for yourself or for a donation."

"But you haven't explained the risks yet," I said.

"Very good, Eve. You're right. I'll be doing that after we do the ultrasound and the pelvic exam. Of course, you won't sign the consents until after that."

"Oh, good," I added.

"And the father must sign a consent, as well."

"The father?" I felt my mouth go dry and I reached for my glass of water.

"Yes, Eve. What we're doing on this is new territory, certainly medically. But also, legally. My lawyer tells me it's important to get the consent of both parents because they may separate at some point, and, of course, both biological parents have an interest in the baby's future."

"That makes sense," I said, wondering how in the heck I'd be able to reach Adam, shock him with all of this, and get him to sign on—like immediately.

"So, can you get a signed consent from your young man before Friday?"

"I'll try. Is the form online?"

"It is. But I'll give you one for the father before you leave, to make it easier. As long as I know it's coming, I really just need it before I begin the surgery on Friday morning. Eve, may I ask whether the young man knows about your plan for Retrieval and Preservation?"

I looked up at her and decided I might as well tell the truth. "He doesn't even know I'm pregnant."

Dr. Hughey closed her eyes for a moment and then smiled at me kindly. She didn't seem to be judging me or anything. She just said, "Of course, it's up to you whether you tell him about your pregnancy, Eve. But I can't do the procedure without his consent. Do you think he'll agree?"

"Yes, Doctor. Of course, I've given this a lot of thought, and he won't have much time to catch up. But, if I can reach him, I think he'll understand why I want to do it."

"If you can reach him?"

"Well, he's doing volunteer work at an orphanage in the Dominican Republic. Plus, he's from Germany so he doesn't have any family near me. But I have an idea how to reach him."

"Dr. Hughey," said Mom, "if there's any problem getting the boy's consent, we'll be sure to let you know right away so you can plan your schedule for Friday. But, assuming Eve's examination works out, and we get the boy's consent, I believe we're ready to be here for the procedure on Friday morning."

"Yes," said Dad. "We'll arrive on Thursday and spend the night in a hotel. I really don't plan to borrow my wife's friend's plane again." He looked at Mom, and she smiled ever so slightly—like the Mona Lisa. The doctor asked if I wanted my parents with me for the examination, and we agreed it would be fine for the ultrasound, but totally unnecessary for the pelvic exam.

I was now nearing the beginning of week 10. In the ultrasound room, Dr. Hughey spread the cool jelly on my tummy and began running the little mouse-like thing over my midsection. A picture started to come in and out of focus. We were all riveted. All of a sudden, we could see it. The embryo was fairly clear. Its head was approximately half the total length of its little body. We could even see some fuzzy hair on its head. Dr. Hughey explained that it was because she was using a 4-D ultrasound that we also were able to see some of the organs through the embryo's translucent skin.

Then she got out the listening device I'd read about. It was faint, but clearly went, "Thump-thump. Thump-thump. Thump-thump." Really fast. That little heartbeat hit me hard. Amazingly, it was the first time it felt real. Although I'd thought of almost nothing else since I'd done the pee test, it had been more of an idea than a being with a heartbeat. But now I'd seen and heard the evidence there was a tiny human growing inside me.

After the pelvic exam, which was nothing compared with what I feared, we all went back into the little conference room. Dr. Hughey told us everything was in order for me to be able to have the Retrieval and Preservation on Friday. She said she believed there was almost no chance she'd damage the embryo or my uterus, in light of the way she'd do the surgery. But, she added, she couldn't guarantee it. Dr. Hughey explained again how I would feel in the hours, days, and months after the laparotomy, and it wasn't that great. And there would be light bleeding and cramping afterwards for up to two weeks. Finally, she talked about the risks of general anesthesia (which Mom had told me all about since she'd had lots of cases where people got brain damage from the anesthetic going wrong), and the risk of infection (which Mom had also told me stories about). Mom said she wasn't hearing anything out of the ordinary and recommended we all sign the consent, if I was still sure it was what I wanted to do. It was funny, but the way she put it forced me to actively make a final decision. I think I'd been floating downstream on my *big idea* since I'd first read about what Dr. Hughey could do.

I liked the thought that the laparotomy would be the best

thing for my cervix, my uterus, and the embryo. And if that meant suffering through six-weeks of discomfort, I was sure I could handle it. But in the back of my mind, I felt certain the fact this would also resolve the argument between my parents carried some weight. So I nodded at them and signed the consent. They both signed after me. Mom signed quickly, but I noticed Dad's pen hovered over the dotted line a couple of beats too long.

Dr. Hughey told us she had one more matter to discuss with us. She explained that her work at this stage was setting the groundwork for more experimentation and analysis, all designed to increase scientific understanding and improve surgical methods for removing and freezing embryos. In order for my surgery to accomplish more than preserving just one embryo, she would need to publish a paper on the procedure. If we consented, it would take her six months to a year to get it published. She would use a pseudonym for my name, probably "Patient X," and would focus on the details of the surgery. But because there was always the chance someone could connect it with me or Adam, she wouldn't attempt to publish without our agreement.

I told her I wasn't sure what to say, but I guessed it would be okay. Mom asked some questions about what medical journals she planned to send it to. Then Dr. Hughey made it easy on us and said she wouldn't even send the release forms to me and Adam until two weeks after my surgery. There was no rush on our decisions, and we should take as long as we needed. She'd really just wanted to explain in person the release forms we'd be getting in the mail. She asked for the orphanage's address so she could also send one to Adam, and Mom found it in her contacts. It was pretty embarrassing to admit we didn't know his last name. But Dr. Hughey showed no reaction when Mom mentioned it. Of course, since I needed his consent before Friday, Adam would know all about what was happening in Toronto long before he'd receive the release for publication.

I was pretty sure I wanted her to publish the article. Otherwise, all of the effort would just be for me and Adam and our embryo, and wouldn't help anybody else. That seemed pretty selfish. Still, I appreciated that I wasn't being asked to make another decision right then.

Dr. Hughey told us the surgery would be at 7:30 a.m. on Friday at the hospital down the street from her building. I would need to be in the surgical waiting room by 6:00 a.m. Apparently, there were a number of things to be done before the moment I'd go into the deep sleep. Mrs. Claus gave us a folder with all of the pre-op instructions for me, and directions to the hospital entrance for in-patient surgeries. The doctor had told us I could be discharged on Sunday if everything went as planned, but that I'd need to stay in bed for a week at home. Mom promised to stay home with me, and said she could do the reports she was behind on much faster from the house than from her office, where she had constant interruptions. I also thought I had a better chance of getting caught up on school work if I were at home for that long. So now, the only piece missing from the puzzle was Adam.

Amazingly, our flight home was on time, getting us back to our house by 11:00 p.m. We were all too exhausted to talk about it anymore that night.

Chapter 17

On Wednesday morning, I looked for Claire at her locker before first period. She was vigorously shaking the snow off her parka. When she saw me, she said, "Hi! Missed you yesterday."

"I know. Sorry I didn't have time to tell you about my trip."

"Where'd you go?"

"Toronto."

"I should've known. Who doesn't ditch classes to make a trip to a foreign country?"

"Yeah."

"What was in Toronto?"

I grabbed her arm to pull her closer, and whispered, "Meet me in the parking lot at lunch. We can talk in my car."

"So, this is about that thing?"

"Yeah." I smiled at her as the bell sounded and we headed in opposite directions for class.

By lunch time, the snow was coming down hard and I had to use my gloved hands to clear a way to the door lock. Seated in the front seat, I immediately put the heater on high, but we had to put up with the cold air blast for the first five minutes. Once we had warm air coming through, we took off our coats and threw them in the back seat. I cracked my window a little so we wouldn't die of carbon monoxide. The car felt igloo-like since we couldn't see anything but white through the windows. Luckily, it seemed more cozy than claustrophobic. I dug out the cheese and cracker packages from my purse and a bottle of cranberry juice to share. I'd hoped it would keep our stomachs from growling all afternoon.

"So? What? Did you decide what you're gonna do? And

why Toronto? What's happening, Eve?"

My mouth was full, so I just smiled in response. For the past two weeks, I'd avoided her questions on my plan, since I really didn't have one. That and the fact I just couldn't take the stress of talking about it constantly. After swallowing a bite of cheese-cracker, I told her the whole story—my parents' fight about what I should do, the results of my research, my discovery of the possibility of cryopreservation of the embryo, and the plan for my surgery on Friday in Toronto.

"First of all, your parents were child-abusing you by making you read six books in two weeks."

"No, they weren't. It was really helpful. I learned tons of things I hadn't known. For example, one doctor who watched an abortion said he saw the fetus actually pull away when the abortionist was inserting the needle near it with the fatal drug in it."

"So?"

"So, it's like what I told little Carmelo and Domingo about the ants they were stepping on. Everything living wants to keep living."

She looked at me steadily, and wasn't smiling. "You're crazy, Eve."

"Why?"

"You're about to have a C-section without getting a baby out of it, risk all the shit that can go wrong in a surgery, take six weeks out of your life to recover, and be out of soccer for this spring and maybe next fall. Right?"

"Yeah."

"And you're going through all this so your folks won't have a fight."

"No."

"So your folks won't split up."

"No."

"Well, the thing is, Eve, it's not necessary."

"What do you mean?"

"What I'm saying is, even if one of your parents would be stupid enough to leave the other over this thing—which won't actually happen—they'd come back. As in, time heals all wounds."

"Wait. I'm not sure I even agree with that cliché. But, Claire, I'm not doing this for them. I've been studying all the arguments about right to life and right to choice, and what the law says, and this feels like a great solution for me. It's not about my parents. This is about me and Adam and the baby."

"Embryo."

"Okay. Embryo."

She ran a couple of tissues through her wet hair, and I was glad I'd put my hood up. "I don't want to sound mean. I really don't, Eve. But how do you know there even *is* a 'me and Adam' now that you've left him in the Dominican Republic? It's like you said, yourself. You'll probably never see him again."

"He wrote a letter."

"Really?"

"Yeah."

"Do you have it with you?"

"Of course. How else can I read it over and over?" I reached down my sweater and pulled it out of my bra.

"May I?"

I hesitated. But I realized this was the best evidence I had of Adam's character and his feelings for me. "Sure."

Once Claire had finished reading it she said, "Wow." She pursed her lips for a few moments, then added, "So, does this make it easier or harder to tell him?"

"Actually, I don't have a choice. The Toronto doctor needs written consent from Adam to do the surgery and preserve the embryo."

"This is some weird shit, Eve."

"I know. As soon as I get home from school, I have to call the orphanage and try to set up a time when Adam can go into town to call me back."

"Why can't they just get him to the phone when you call?"

"He'll probably be working with the boys or doing something else for the orphanage. I'm going to need at least a half hour to get him caught up on all of this, and I can't tie up their only phone that long. Also, he'll need to be at one of the internet cafes to receive the consent form and get it back to Dr. Hughey."

"What do you think he'll say?"

"I don't know exactly. But I can't wait to talk with him." I smiled at Claire as I handed her the last of the juice, and we finished off the crackers. We reached back for our coats and braced ourselves to leave the cozy igloo for the snowstorm.

***

As soon as I got home from school, I fished through my folder of information on the orphanage until I found their emergency number. I'd forgotten how to do the out-of- country code, so I called the international operator for instructions. I reached the orphanage on my first try. Luckily, Jan answered, so she knew who-the-heck I was. She agreed to have Adam take a break and walk into town to call me back, collect, on our land-line. Jan said she thought he'd be able to get to it within a couple of hours.

I didn't move from my chair in the family room for an hour, until the phone rang. Even though I'd been waiting for the call, I was startled. I suddenly realized that I'd zoned out and hadn't given a minute's thought to how I would break all of the news to Adam.

"Hello. This is the international operator. Will you accept charges for a call from Adam Wagner?" She pronounced the "w" like a "v". So that was his last name.

"Of course I will."

"Eve! Are you okay?"

The absolute panic in his voice called for quick and emphatic response. "I'm fine, Adam."

"Oh, thank God. I've been very worried since I got the message to call. So, you're really okay?"

I felt instantly relaxed and soothed to hear his voice, and his concern for me. "Yes, Adam. It's great to hear your voice. How are you?"

"I'm well. I miss you very much though. It hasn't been nearly as enjoyable here since you left. Or, for that matter, before you arrived."

"I miss you, too. So much."

"So, have you called just to visit?"

How I wished I could say yes. "Not exactly."

"What then? What's happened, Eve?"

"I know this'll come as a shock, but the night we made love…well, we got me pregnant."

"Oh, no." His words came out slowly. Deliberately.

"I know. Not exactly something we expected."

"No, Eve. It's not that. I must confess something."

That put me immediately into panic mode. Was it something horrible like a girlfriend back in Germany? Maybe he was married. My heart was racing, but I tried to sound calm. "Okay. What is it?"

"Well, that night, when I removed the condom…it felt odd. Almost brittle. I've been hoping you were okay—not pregnant. But I did walk over to the tobacco shop near the English Institute where I bought the thing. I asked the man how long he'd had those on the shelf."

"What did he say?"

"He said, 'Not long—maybe five or six years.' Then he explained that no one buys them anymore except tourists because the government gives them away."

"Well, that explains it. I was wondering how we could be so lucky to be in the 2%."

"I am so sorry, Eve."

"It's not your fault."

"When did you find out?"

"Almost four weeks ago."

"Really? Why didn't you call me?"

"I just didn't want to worry you with it. I had a lot of studying and reading to get through to decide what I wanted to do."

"But why are you saying 'what *I* wanted to do' rather than 'what *we* wanted to do'? I don't understand."

He sounded so hurt it hit me immediately. I'd been very foolish to have excluded Adam. And this call was not going to go well. "I guess I assumed you'd support whatever I wanted to do. And it was definitely a hard decision."

"Why do you say, 'it was'? Have you already made up your mind?"

How I wished I could deny this. But I had no choice. I had to get his consent in the next two days, so there was no point hiding what I'd done. "Yes. But it's kind of a long story."

"Okay."

I was so nervous that I told Adam every single thing: how I'd learned I was pregnant and confided in Claire, how she saw no solution other than an abortion, how strongly Mom believed I should have the baby while Dad thought it would be crazy for me to not have an abortion, how I'd studied the six books, and realized both sides of the debate were correct, how I'd had the idea to see if this might be treated with an IVF and freezing kind of approach and found a respected doctor who was doing just that, how we'd met with Dr. Hughey, who was well-credentialed and well-regarded and seemed like a good person, and how Dr. Hughey needed Adam's written consent for the Retrieval and Preservation which was scheduled for Friday.

Adam didn't say anything for awhile, until I thought maybe we'd been disconnected. "Adam, are you there?"

"Yes. I'm sorry, Eve. I was just processing it."

"What do you think?"

"Honestly, I'm having trouble getting past why you didn't trust me enough to tell me."

"I just didn't want to put any pressure on you, or to worry you."

"Yes. You said that before."

My problem wasn't that I couldn't think of a good way to say it. My problem was that I'd been wrong not to tell Adam, and I couldn't undo my mistake. All that was left to do was apologize. "I'm sorry, Adam. You're right. I should've told you first."

"Eve, I don't mind that you told your best friend or your parents before you told me. They were right there with you, while I wasn't. What bothers me is that you waited so long after that to tell me." He paused. "Would you ever have told me if Dr. Hughey didn't need my consent?"

"Of course. I would've told you before the surgery."

"But you didn't."

"You don't understand, Adam. I didn't know the surgery was even possible for me until yesterday afternoon in Toronto. I had to go to school today and called you the moment I got home." I thought that timing actually sounded pretty good. Unfortunately, Adam saw right through it.

"But you did the research on cryopreservation this past weekend. Why not call me before you went to Toronto? Did my opinion mean nothing to you?"

Now I paused for a minute to get my thoughts together. I hadn't been prepared for his questions or how disappointed he was in me. I took a long breath. "Adam, I made a terrible mistake not talking to you about this along the way. Your opinion means everything to me. I just wanted to try to find a good solution before I told you. Protecting you from worry was a ridiculous idea. You don't need protecting. I never meant to hurt you. Can you forgive me?"

"I will try, Eve. Please email to me the form and I will sign it and send it to the doctor." He gave me an email address. His voice grew quieter as he spoke, like he was fading away. Then he said, "Good luck with your procedure, Eve."

"So, I guess we'll start writing in mid-August, like we planned." Since Adam didn't say anything, I added, "Right?"

He definitely hesitated before saying yes.

"Bye, Adam."

"Goodbye, Eve."

He had sounded so sad that it broke my heart. Having sabotaged my happiness with Adam, I felt absolutely drained. The phone rang and I uttered a little prayer that it was Adam calling back.

A woman's voice. "Hello, Eve?"

"Yes."

"This is Ms. Griffin from school."

"Oh, hi."

"Eve, I see you're planning to be out on Friday and through the following week for medical reasons."

"Yes. That's true."

"You know, you'll need a doctor's note when you return."

"Yes, I know. I'll have one."

"Are you okay?"

"Actually, I'm having a laparotomy." Mom had prepped me on how to handle the question—with answers that were technically true. "I have something that's apparently not a cyst. So, they want to go in and have a look around. It could be an endomitrioma. Do you know what that is?"

"As a matter of fact, I do. My sister had one. Same surgery. I think it was a six-week recovery."

"That's me."

"Well, I'm so sorry to hear it, Eve. Good luck with your

procedure. Let me know if I can do anything for you."

"Thank you so much. But my friend, Claire, will pick up my assignments and drop off my work with my teachers. So I think I'm all set."

"Good luck, dear."

"Thanks, Ms. Griffin. Goodbye."

"Goodbye."

Now, Mom and I would just have to come up with a logical explanation for why my doctor's note would be from a Canadian doctor.

I was so distraught over screwing up with Adam that I had to do something. I grabbed one of Mom's legal pads and began to write a letter to him. My main theme was how sorry I was and how much his forgiveness would mean to me. Just writing the thing did make me feel a little better. But I knew it wouldn't be picked up until the next morning and would probably take two weeks to get to Adam. Having it done and in the mailbox was only a tiny comfort.

Mom also got home a little early and came straight up to my room to find out if I'd been able to reach Adam and what he'd said. She needed to confirm for Dr. Hughey's office that the consent was on the way. I kept it simple. "He was surprised but agreed to sign. I think I hurt his feelings by waiting 'til the last minute to tell him."

"Well sweetie, it's been a tough situation. You two can talk about it more after you get it behind you." She smiled.

"Yeah. Thanks, Mom." I didn't smile back.

Chapter 18

The next day was Thursday and we were off to Toronto again. This time we didn't take any chances. Mom actually booked us on two different airlines, and then cancelled the later one once we'd boarded the earlier one. We were safe and sound in our hotel room, only minutes from the hospital, by 5:00 p.m. We all agreed to have a room service dinner rather than risk adding any stress to our day. Of course, we usually loved exploring new cities together, but I think we all realized we couldn't spare a single ounce of anxiety since every bit we had was already wrapped around what I'd be doing the next morning. I couldn't eat after 9:00 p.m. anyway, per my pre-op instructions. So we had Caesar salads and French bread, and shared a tiramisu for dessert. We all watched the 6:00 news, but I'd bet none of us could say what any of it had been about.

For my part, the worry was equal parts my surgery and Adam. I felt so stupid for the way I'd handled it with him. And all the while, I'd been so proud of how studiously and objectively I'd dealt with the decision. I think Mom and Dad probably assumed my quiet mood was all about the operation, and I didn't correct them. But, after a while, I got tired of kicking myself for my stupidity, especially since there was nothing I could do about it. Dad said good night and went to their bedroom after the news, and Mom opened her laptop to read her lawyer stuff in the living room area of our suite. She sat on the pull-out couch that would later become my bed. I decided to text Claire with an update.

Me: Hi! Made it to T. hotel
Claire: Good. R u nervous?

Me: Not 2 much. Bummed I screwed up with Adam. I'm so stupid

Claire: U r not stupid, miss straight A's. U may b brilliant

Me: Hardly. U were right. Should've told him sooner

Claire: Boys r tricky. Hard 2 know what 2 do.

Me: No. This is about treating people fairly. Should've known. I've been a people for 16 yrs

Claire: What will u do?

Me: Don't know. I'll keep thinking

Claire: Good luck tomorrow!

Me: Thanks :)

Claire: Call me after. As soon as u get into your room

Me: I'll try. Maybe text

Claire: No. Have 2 hear your voice

Me: OK. Will do

Claire: Good nite!

Me: Nite!

I worked on a school assignment for a while, but I couldn't focus very well. After a half hour or so, I reached into my backpack and pulled out a paperback on constellations I'd found in the school library. My plan was to memorize facts until I was tired enough to go to sleep. I stayed away from the constellations Adam had told me about, since I doubted I could handle those. But I'd gotten interested in the myths and thought they'd make a good memory exercise. I started with Pisces because it was Claire's sign. I tried to read silently, but apparently my lips were moving. "Pisces represents the fish into which Aphrodite (also considered Venus) and her son

Eros (also considered Cupid) transformed themselves in order to escape the horrible earthborn giant, Typhoeus. The mother and son were bathing on the banks of the Euphrates River that day and took on the shapes of a pair of fish to escape…."

Mom was looking at me. She said, "What're you doing?"

I rolled my eyes at myself before answering. "Memorizing."

"What?"

"Oh, it's just stuff on the myths about the constellations."

"For school?"

"No." I was embarrassed I couldn't handle my stress without resorting to something so silly.

She tilted her head. "So, why memorize it?"

"I know this'll sound crazy, Mom. But if I keep my brain occupied like this, it kinda takes up all the room in there, so there's no space for worries."

"It's not crazy, Eve. In fact, it's a pretty good idea to memorize. I wish I'd thought of that when I had to calm my mind."

"About my surgery?"

"Oh no. This was ages ago. There was a year right after I'd started practicing law, when I got so stressed worrying about all my files that I'd go home to my apartment and focus on my bedroom door knob."

"Are you serious?"

"Oh yes. And I couldn't just look at it. I had to chant, 'door knob, door knob, door knob…'"

I laughed, then quickly realized my reaction wasn't very sympathetic. "Sorry, Mom. That must've been horrible."

"No, it's fine, Eve. It does sound funny now. I mean, if I'd been as creative as you I could've memorized the history of the doorknob, or something else that might come in handy in a trivia contest someday." She smiled. "The thing is, sweetie, we do what we need to do in order to survive. My better option at the time would've been to tell the partner I was working with that I had too many files. But I didn't want to show any weakness, so I took it home to the door knob instead." She laughed. "But there is something that's been bothering me. And I think I'd be smarter to just talk with you about it than to start focusing on door knobs again."

"About my surgery?"

"No. About my parenting."

"What do you mean?"

She hesitated, then let out an audible sigh. "I've been kicking myself for not suggesting you consider starting on the pill."

"Oh, Mom. It's not your fault."

"I know. It's just that I put way too much stock in the fact that I knew you weren't dating." She smiled. "I did have a plan, you know."

"What plan?"

"Well, if you did start dating again in high school, I was going to sit you down and tell you the reasons I thought you probably shouldn't want to have sex yet."

"Oh." I immediately felt embarrassed, and a little bit judged.

Apparently, Mom could tell. She said, "Wait. Let me finish."

"Okay."

"But, I was going to tell you, if you *were* planning to have sex, I wanted to help you get birth control pills."

"That was a good plan, Mom." I gazed at her, appreciative of the effort she put into this stuff.

"Yeah. But not quite good enough." I saw tears were
forming in her eyes.

I loved her so much at that moment. "You're a great
mom. And I'm fine." I walked over and leaned down to give
her a hug. "I love you."

"I love you, too, sweetie." This felt especially intense.
Mom was amazing in every way but had never been especially
sentimental.

I had an idea I wanted to talk with her about, so I sat
down next to her on the couch. She turned to face me, and we
were only about two feet apart. "I've been thinking about all
the scientific work needed to prevent pregnancies, and to make
things like I'm doing tomorrow a lot easier. And I just think it
should be done mainly by women."

"Interesting. Why so?" asked Mom. I couldn't help noticing again how beautiful she was. Just sitting in her t-shirt and
sweatpants, talking with me. I thought the best word for her
was elegant.

"I know this is probably sexist, but men have been in
charge for so long—and we haven't gotten any of what I'm
talking about. So things couldn't get any worse if women were
the ones pushing the science."

"I can see that."

"I've also been thinking about you, and how hard it must
be for you."

"Your pregnancy?"

"Sure. But I was actually talking about how hard it must
be to be a pro-life feminist."

"It is. A lot of people assume I'm a simpleton, just following yesterday's sermon."

"Yeah. It really surprised Claire when I told her you're pro-life."

"The hardest thing about arguing my thoughts is just getting anybody to listen. My views are based on morality, not theology. The truth is, Eve, most people aren't as open minded as you are."

"I know. I really think it's because both sides are right that neither can hear the other very well. If we could accept that, we could move on to looking for the answers. And we could look in the right place--science and medicine."

"You convinced me on Sunday evening." She smiled.

Then something struck me. "Have you ever thought that maybe we're still where we are on this 'cause the male leadership, maybe even unconsciously, wants to keep women divided?"

"Well, whether conscious or not, things have certainly evolved that way. I think you're right, Eve. The whole debate has made women the losers."

"As in, 'patsies'?"

She thought for a moment. "Yeah. Kind of."

"Well, shit." My hand jerked to cover my mouth. Too late. I was starting to get a little loose with swears and decided to try harder not to irritate her with it. "Sorry. But what can we do about it?"

"What you're doing tomorrow. And by your becoming a scientist or a doctor."

"I'd love to work on improving birth control. And the stuff Dr. Hughey's doing would be freaking fascinating—even if it weren't about me. I think it could save a lot of lives. But none of this will work 'til we women stop fighting about it and work together. We're sabotaging ourselves, aren't we?"

She nodded slowly. "Yes. We are."

"I know a little bit about how easy it is to sabotage yourself."

"How so?"

"Oh, it's nothing."

"There's a lot of work to be done. And I think you're right. The starting place has to be respectful conversations among women. I believe you'll work on these things, sweetie. You're exactly the kind of woman who can really make a difference."

"Thanks. I don't know what kind of woman I am. But I can promise you this. If I don't, it won't be for lack of trying. Because the way things are for women really sucks."

"I know."

I looked at my watch and told Mom I wanted to go ahead and get to bed since we had a 6:00 a.m. check-in at the hospital. She helped me with the pull-out bed and we got the linens arranged. I ran into the bathroom to get ready and then slid under the covers, feeling exhausted. She kissed me goodnight like she used to do when I was little.

Sure enough, now that my memorizing and talking with Mom were over, the worries moved in. Thoughts bumped around wildly in my head. I was angry with Adam that he hadn't been more supportive and acted like this was more about his feelings than my pregnancy. Then I was shocked at my own callousness. How many times had I said, "Half the chromosomes are the man's"? If I really believed the man should have equal responsibility, didn't it stand to reason he should have equal input into the decision?

Then I sat bolt upright because something new had hit me smack in the face. I hadn't asked Adam for his opinion! Even when I finally told him everything Claire and my parents and I had analyzed, I'd moronically not asked what he thought--what he'd do if it were all up to him. I became even more miserable—something I didn't think was possible, and got a sudden splitting headache. How in the world did I expect my apology to be accepted when I'd been a complete, insensitive jerk while making it? It struck me as amazing I'd felt so proud of how I'd handled everything, when I'd thoroughly screwed up with the one person who should have been my partner in it.

I refused to take anything for my headache because I wasn't sure it wouldn't hurt the embryo. It was the least I could do. I knew I had to write another letter to Adam, to apologize again…only differently. But there was something else bothering me. The thing was, there was still time. Only a few hours. But I could call the orphanage's emergency number to make sure Adam was really okay with it. I doubted I'd reach him in the middle of the night, but I had to try.

I tiptoed into the little kitchenette so I wouldn't wake my parents, and used my cell phone. Luckily, when I'd called Adam before, I'd added the orphanage number to my contacts. The phone rang, probably ten times, and then went into voice-mail. I left a brief message asking that Adam call my cell number, collect, as soon as possible. I doubted he'd even receive the message by the time of my surgery. All those worries were popping in my mind, my head hurt, and I was completely wound up with anxiety. I would never admit it to Mom and

Dad, but I still hadn't fallen asleep when my alarm went off at 5:00 a.m. I'm sure I looked like crap, but my parents didn't say anything. They let me shower first, and it did refresh me a little. I brushed my teeth, then put on a little makeup for no logical reason. I pulled my hair back in a low ponytail, thinking I didn't want it to get in the way of the anesthesia tubes. I'd packed my purple orphanage t-shirt for the occasion, in spite of the fact it definitely wasn't t-shirt weather. I pulled on my jeans and stepped into my Uggs.

Mom and Dad dressed quickly and said they'd grab a bite while I was in surgery so I wouldn't have to watch them eat, while I couldn't. Mom reached into the closet and pulled out our wool coats and scarves. She and Dad grabbed their laptops. When I raised my eyebrows, Mom said, "There could be a lot of downtime, Eve. We may as well use it productively." We headed downstairs, where the hotel's concierge explained it was only a two-block walk to the hospital, and it was a lovely, brisk morning. He also offered to arrange for a cab for us if we preferred. We all agreed that a walk would do us good. It was 5:45 a.m., dark, and the city streets were just beginning to come to life. The air felt colder than "brisk," and the wind was whipping us fiercely. I was relieved to step into the revolving doors of the hospital's main lobby

Chapter 19

Someone gave us directions to the inpatient surgery waiting room and we walked down three long hallways to get there. The whole place had a clean, fresh feel to it--what I breathed in was more like flowers than Lysol. And all of the hospital staff we passed smiled and said good morning. Even the other people, probably visitors or arriving patients like me, were super friendly. I assumed they were all Canadians.

There were already probably a dozen people sitting on the chairs and couches as we entered the large room. Televisions hung on two opposite walls of the space, but the volume was turned off so you had to read the captions, which weren't keeping pace with the speakers' mouths. I was looking to see if there was any "breaking news." While trying to quickly read about an avalanche in Italy, I heard the receptionist say, "Gehraghty? And did you say her first name is Eve?" She was speaking to a young man standing at her desk wearing a too small tan suit. It took my head a few moments to catch up with what my eyes were seeing. My heart did a little leap, then my whole body relaxed as though I'd been holding my breath for days and could finally exhale. I walked up to him from behind, tapped him on the shoulder, and said, "Adam."

He turned and whispered, "Eve!" I fell into his arms and we hugged and I cried until I heard the receptionist loudly clear her throat.

She smiled kindly, then spoke. "Would you like to get registered? And then there should be plenty of time to visit with your friend before the nurses are ready for you. Will that work for all of you?"

Mom stepped forward and said, "Yes. It will. Thank you so much." I was trying to wipe away the tears covering my cheeks. The receptionist pointed me and my parents to a small office, just behind her counter.

Before we headed there, I turned to Adam and managed to choke out, "Thanks for coming." Then I nodded to my parents and added, "Mom, Dad, this is Adam. Adam, my parents, Jennifer and Dan Gehraghty."

He reached out his hand to shake, with Mom first and then with Dad, while saying, "It is a great pleasure to meet you, Mr. and Mrs. Gehraghty."

Mom spent a moment taking in Adam in the weirdly small suit. Then she smiled at him warmly and said, "It's nice to meet you too, Adam."

Dad just stared at him until I said, "Dad?" He then swallowed audibly and nodded at Adam.

We turned to head to the small office. As we entered the tiny room, Mom whispered to me, "I like him."

Adam took a seat in the waiting room while we reviewed the paperwork with the middle-aged woman in the office. Then Dad handed her a credit card and said, "Whatever it is, just put it on here." He smiled at me and patted my hand. A wave of embarrassment washed over me—at my privilege. I couldn't help but think of the millions of women for whom such a thing would never happen. I was ashamed for being so lucky.

The office woman told us, now that my registration was complete, the wait could be up to an hour. Apparently, all of the surgical patients needed to get their paperwork done before they would start coming for any of us. So she sent us back to the waiting room, and Adam stood as we entered. Mom took control of the situation. "Eve, why don't you and Adam find a spot in a quiet corner to talk. Your father and I will have plenty of time to visit with him while you're having the procedure."

"Thanks, Mom."

"That is very kind, Mrs. Gehraghty," said Adam. She smiled and nodded. My parents walked to the other side of the room and chose seats so their backs were to us. Adam took my hand and led me to a corner spot, just large enough for two of the beige, upholstered chairs. He sat directly across from me with a tiny, round wooden table between us.

I said, "Adam, how on earth did you get here so quickly? I just called you at the orphanage at 2 a.m."

"By then, I was sound asleep in the hostel down the street from here."

"But, how? How could you afford it? I don't understand how you managed it."

He smiled that gentle smile of his and said, "Do you want to hear the whole story?"

"Yes. Please tell me everything." My memory of Adam's appeal to me had not done him justice. My urge was to hug him and kiss him, but I made myself focus on what he was telling me.

"The night when you first called me with the news of your pregnancy…"

"Wednesday."

"Yes. On Wednesday night, I was in turmoil. So I just slipped out after dark and made my way to our spot on the hill. As I was studying the Big Dipper and then shifting my focus to see Big Bear, the thought hit me that I had only been looking at what you'd told me from my own point of view."

"Well, that was logical."

"No. No, it wasn't, Eve. There was another way to focus on it that I had been ignoring—your perspective. So I tried to imagine what it must have felt like for you to learn that you were pregnant—after having sex exactly one time. So far away from me, and with little means to reach me. Knowing your parents would be at odds over what you should do. Then studying conflicting theories about the morality of abortion and a woman's right to control her own body. And the whole time, feeling that what you were going through was so painful you did not want to inflict the same pain on me. Your kind impulse was not unreasonable, Eve. Also, I kicked myself for being so disappointed in you for not telling me sooner—when I hadn't told you about the brittle condom. I could've reached out to you just as easily. I am truly sorry for the way I reacted."

"Oh, God, thank you, Adam! I've been feeling so horrible about how I wasn't thinking enough of your feelings." I paused, then added, "Of course, I should've done the same thing. If I'd just put myself in your shoes, I would've realized that, painful or not, you would definitely want to know. I hope you can forgive me for getting that so wrong."

He smiled at me again. "Of course I can, Eve. What you did out of love cannot be dismissed simply because I would have preferred you had done it another way."

I smiled and nodded my head. I took a deep breath to admit more stupidity. "The worst thing is, even when I finally called you, I still didn't ask for your opinion." He just continued to look at me, and bit his lip ever so slightly. "So, I'd really like to ask for it now. I know the timing is ridiculous, with my operation starting in less than an hour. But, the thing is, Adam,

I really do still have an open mind. I tried to make the best decision—in all the circumstances. But, I could still probably be swayed if you have a strong preference and explain it to me."

Adam reached for my hands and held both of them as he spoke. "Abortion is legal in Germany, and, frankly, I'd never before given it a lot of thought. I have always been pro-choice. I believed the woman should decide. But, after you shared your thoughts with me, I tried to change my focus for once to the embryo. Its 'right to a future,' as you put it. And everything you said to me on the telephone also made sense. It is a very troubling issue. I know I would never want to see abortion made a crime—for the woman or her doctor. But, once a woman is pregnant, unintentionally, and where it would be better for her, and for society, that she not have a child at that time –well, she must have rights, too. So it was amazing to hear of the third alternative you have found. It is so encouraging that science has found a way to end a pregnancy without ending the embryo. Like the way you will be solving today the problem we face."

When Adam said, 'we,' I lost it. Tears flowed uncontrollably down my cheeks. As I've mentioned, I don't like to cry. My main complaint about it is that I don't ever want anyone to think I do it on purpose to be manipulative, because I don't. But there I sat, with my face totally soaked with tears. Adam came to my side, knelt by my chair, and dried my face with a tissue from his jacket pocket. "So, are you really okay with what I am about to do, Adam?"

He smiled. "More than okay. I am in awe of you. You didn't flinch. You jumped in and studied your options, identified an innovative solution, and accepted it in spite of risk to you, and the certainty of the need for a long recovery. You are willing to sacrifice to make it work for yourself, and for us. Eve, I support your decision completely."

"I am so happy to hear that. I really think it's the best thing."

"I know you do. If you had just wanted to be rid of the pregnancy, you could've had an out-patient abortion and been on your way home the same afternoon. What you are doing is not only brilliant, it's also brave and generous. You really are an amazing woman, Eve." Adam leaned over and kissed me softly on the lips and then returned to his chair.

I felt like a huge weight had been lifted from my shoulders. The headache I'd had all morning evaporated. I smiled at him, then whispered, "Thanks so much. That means the world to me." Now that I had his apology and his forgiveness, my mood lightened instantly. I cocked my head and smiled. "So, now will you tell me why you're wearing a suit that belongs to one of your little brothers?"

He laughed. "I was hoping you hadn't noticed."

"Not possible."

"Here's what happened. Once I realized how wrong I had been about focusing only on myself, I wanted desperately to get to Toronto to see you before the operation. So I hurried down the hill, ran into the bunkhouse, and woke Gerhard in the middle of the night. I told him what was happening, and he looked at me like I was a madman. So, I made it simple. 'Gerhard, I need to get to Toronto tomorrow morning. Do you think your mother will help me?' 'Of course. She will if she can, Adam. You must know she thinks of you as a second son. Really, I am not following your story, but, yes, I will call my mother now to see what she can do.'"

"We ran down to the office, Gerhard in only his boxers, and tried the door. Of course, it was locked. So we banged on the director's door to request the key. Gerhard said something like, 'I need to use the emergency phone to call my mother.' Of course, this was technically true, but I am sure it gave the director the impression that it was his mother who was in some distress. Anyway, Gerhard got the key and was able to reach his mother in Germany. It was 2:00 a.m. where we were, and 8:00 a.m. in Cologne. He assured her everything was fine, but explained that I needed a round trip buddy pass to Toronto, with my outbound flight that very morning. Yesterday, actually. She agreed to get right on her computer and let us know as soon as she had something."

"What's a buddy pass?"

"It is one of the perks of working for an airline. The employee can get free passes for relatives and friends. It's just that the friend must fly standby—and hope for an open seat. You see, Gerhard's mother works as a reservationist for a large airline. She had told me to be sure to ask if I ever needed a flight and she would do what she could. I'd asked her about my trip in November, but there were no open seats then. So, she looked for me again. Oh, and there's a dress code for the 'buddies' which is strictly enforced."

"Getting us to the explanation for your suit?"

"Exactly." He paused and looked over my shoulder. "Eve, there is a water cooler just behind you. Are you allowed a drink?"

"No, thanks. I'd rather just keep talking with you."

"Well, Gerhard's mother got the pass for me. But the flight leaves only three hours from then. And, of course, there are no open seats on the later flights. So, I said, 'Great! I will take it.' But then Gerhard reminded me I needed a suit or at least a sport coat to board on a buddy-pass. And all I have at the orphanage are shorts and purple t-shirts."

"And it's the middle of the night." I shook my head in disbelief. "So, where did you find this beautiful, ill-fitting, summer suit?"

"I had to think quickly. Who would have a suit or a sport coat, and also would know me well enough to loan it to me?"

"Who?"

"There is only one possibility. Vincent Garcia."

"Who's Vincent Garcia? Wait! Not the man who runs the tobacco shop where you bought the thing?"

"No. Although I would say he owes us a favor. No. Vincent Garcia is the director of the English Institute. I have talked with him several times, and have remembered he wears a suit to work every day—even when it is quite hot."

"So, you called him ?"

"Unfortunately, I did not have his home number. Even though he lives just behind the Institute complex, I think he must have a separate number for his home because no one answered at the Institute."

"So, what? You knocked on his door in the middle of the night?"

"Actually, yes. Gerhard agreed to go with me so that at least one of would live to explain what we'd been up to if Mr. Garcia happened to shoot the other one of us."

"Always good to have a backup plan."

"Yes. That is what we thought."

"But, seriously, weren't you afraid?"

"Seriously, yes. I was. Once we knocked on his door, I had this terrible feeling of being trapped—no turning back."

"What did you say to him?"

"First, I apologized profusely. Then I made it very simple. I just said I must wear a suit to fly to Canada, but I have no dress clothing with me. So, could I please borrow one. Then I will have it cleaned and return it soon."

"And he just handed over this suit—just like that?"

"Yes. We walked into his living room. He went to the back of the house and returned with this cotton suit, a shirt and a tie. He said, 'Put them on, Adam.' And I did. As you see, Vincent is three inches shorter than I…shorter arms, too." He laughed. "Worse than that, he gave me this pair of brown shoes—which fit fine. But you have surely noticed I have gained two inches in height." I looked at the shoes. They weren't like platforms. More like cowboy boots with high heels. I grimaced. Adam laughed again, and I was reminded of how much I adored that unrestrained bubbling sound.

"And they let you board the flight looking like this?"

"Yes. Yes. I had followed their dress code. So there was really nothing they could do about the deficiencies in my tailoring."

"That's amazing. When did you get here?"

"I had to fly through Newark, and the flight from there to Toronto was delayed. So I did not reach my hostel until 11:00 p.m. Let me just say that my clothing is not terribly out of place at the hostel. I will tell you about it later." He let out a long breath, and sort of gazed at me. "But, I made it, Eve. I had learned from the hospital what time surgery patients had to check in. I knew I would get to see you—if your parents didn't toss me out. I slept well. I would see you this morning. I was finally relaxed."

"But how did you even know what hospital I'd be in?"

"It was all in the release I signed. All the details were there."

"I still can't believe you're sitting here with me. I'm finally starting to feel relaxed, too. Loved. Cared for. And about to be in the hands of a doctor I trust. Thank you so much for everything, Adam. I'll be fine. Can you be with me when I wake up?"

"If it is permitted, I will be there."

The receptionist called out my name and all four of us walked up to her counter. She said my parents and Adam could go with me into pre-op. Adam kissed me on the cheek very gently and said, "Mr. and Mrs. Gehraghty, you should be with Eve now. I will wait here during the operation. Perhaps you could ask them if I may be with Eve afterward."

"Thank you, Adam. That's very considerate. And we'll certainly ask," said Mom.

"Yes. That sounds good, Adam. We'll be back shortly," said Dad. Mom already acted like she was comfortable with Adam. But Dad seemed pretty guarded. Still, I was confident he'd like Adam too once he got to know him.

We hugged, and Adam whispered, "Good luck. I love you."

I smiled at him, and could only think to say, "Me, too."

We went into a small, curtained area where I slipped into a hospital gown before my parents were allowed in. As I lay on a cart-like thing on wheels, a nurse covered me with a heavenly toasty electric blanket. Then the echo chamber began. At least four people came in, separately, to ask me identical questions about me, general health issues, allergies, what I was having done, etc. From what I could make out, the first was the anesthesiologist's assistant, then the anesthesiologist, then the surgical assistant, and finally, Dr. Hughey. Although they were all very Canadian, I was happiest to see Dr. Hughey.

"Good morning, Eve. Mr. and Mrs. Gehraghty. How is everyone this fine morning?"

"A little nervous," confessed Mom. This surprised me since she was normally the most calm one in the family.

Dad said, "I'll admit to some butterflies, too." It made me sad that they were nervous.

Dr. Hughey smiled at them and then turned to me. "Are you a bit jittery as well, Eve?"

"Actually, doctor, I'd say I'm placid, bordering on serene." I smiled.

"Any particular reason for that?"

"Well, seeing you again, I remember how confident you make me feel--how much I trust you. I'm very ready."

"Well, thank you very much. But, I must tell you, Eve, your parents can't help themselves. I'm afraid being a parent means worrying. It goes with the territory."

"Of course. I see that."

"Yes. I believe you do." Then, looking back at my parents, she said, "You may say your goodbyes now. The surgery will take approximately two hours. I'll give you a call in the waiting room as soon as I've finished. And then, once she's wakened from the anesthetic, you may come into recovery to be with her."

Dad cleared his throat and said, "May her friend, Adam, be with her at that time?"

"Ah, the father! He came all the way from the Dominican Republic?"

"Yes," I said, proudly. "He's the other reason I feel so good."

"Then, of course he should be with you." She nodded to the nurse, who started fidgeting with my cart to get the wheels rolling while Dr. Hughey walked into the hallway.

First Mom, and then Dad, kissed me on the cheek and told me they loved me. When Dad leaned down, I pulled him closer and whispered into his ear, "Please be nice to Adam." He winked at me, which he never does. I stuck out my little finger for a pinky-swear, and he did it! We hadn't done that together since I was like six years old. I said, "I love you both," and gave them a thumbs-up and an overly big smile.

After my conversation with Adam, and then feeling my parents' unconditional love, I really did feel pretty relaxed and ready to drift into unconsciousness...to fulfill my plan.

Chapter 20

"Eve? Can you open your eyes?" It was Dr. Hughey's voice. I blinked my eyes open and made out her shape through a haze. She came into focus, and I saw I was lying under very bright, fluorescent lights. My head felt like it was swaying.

"Where am I?"

"You're in recovery, Eve."

"Oh, good. How'd I do?" I saw that there was an IV needle in my left arm, and vaguely remembered that it had been stuck in me before the lights went out.

"Just fine. We're just going to keep an eye on you to be sure your bleeding is at an acceptable level."

"Right."

"A couple of weeks of spotting would be expected."

"Okay. So, where are my parents? And where's Adam?" My head was still wobbly.

"They're all in the waiting room. Your parents will be able to come see you very soon. And I've made sure that Adam will be allowed in, as well."

"Thanks." All of a sudden, I remembered what was going on. "Wait! How did our embryo do?" I'm not positive, but I think my speech was slurred.

"Very well. Textbook perfect embryo and placenta, actually. I'll let the nurse know your visitors may come in now." She started to leave and then turned back to me. "Everything really did work out as I'd hoped, Eve." She smiled, then left the curtained area and pulled the drape closed behind her.

I shut my eyes and nodded off, in spite of the entire area being brightly lit, and lots of loud hospital noises pulsating in the background. I have no idea how much time passed. Some-one touched my shoulder and I heard Mom say, "Eve. We're here."

I had to make my way up out of the haze again. Mom and Dad were standing by my bed. "Hi guys. Dr. Hughey told me I'm okie-dokie!" I think I gave them a goofy smile.

"Yes. You did great, sweetie," said Mom, and then she leaned down to kiss me on the cheek.

"And the doctor lady said the embyro's good, too. I'm so happy!"

"She told us," said Dad. "That's really good news. So, how're you feeling?"

"A little foggy, Dad. But I guess the good thing is, since I'm still under the influence, I don't really have any pain." I paused. "I sound weird to myself. Do I sound weird to you guys?"

"You sound just like you should—a little groggy," said Mom. "I'm glad you don't have pain yet, sweetie, but I think some will be paying you a visit later."

"Yeah. The doc warned me tomorrow should be the worst. I'm not afraid of pain," I said in a voice I meant to sound macho. "The important thing is, it worked!" I beamed.

"I agree with that," said Mom. "But when you do start to hurt, ask for the medicine you need. You've done enough. Don't be a martyr about the pain. Okay?"

"Sure, Mommy! But I don't want a bunch of narcotics floating around inside me trying to get me hooked on drugs." I laughed, then added, "It's bad enough I'm hooked on pho-nics!"

Dad snorted a laugh, and then narrowed his eyes and

looked at me like I wasn't quite right.

"That would be fine," said Mom. "Just listen to your body, sweetie."

"I will."

"Shall we ask Adam to come in?" said Dad.

"Yes!"

They smiled at each other as they swept through the curtain and the little rings made a scraping noise against the rod. In a minute, Adam was peeking his head through, tentatively, like he was hoping he'd chosen the right curtain. "Eve!" He came up to my bedside and gave me a gentle kiss on the lips. He whispered, "I got worried when it had been almost two hours—with no word. But just as I got up to pace, Dr. Hughey called your mother in the waiting room to tell her everything had gone well." Just seeing Adam sent a wave of calm and joy through me. "How do you feel?"

"Really fine. I don't have much pain yet! And I'm so happy our embryo did great, too." He took my hand and smiled his soft, warm smile. Since I was dying to know how they'd gotten along, I said, "So, did you get to visit with my 'rents?"

"What?"

I rolled my eyes. "My parents."

"Got it. Yes, we got to know each other a bit. They even forgave me for the suit! And once Dr. Hughey called your mother in the waiting room, we all hugged."

I let out a long, overly-dramatic sigh of relief. After a quick rustling of the curtain, Dr. Hughey walked in with my parents and they all stood around my bed. The doctor smiled at everyone. "I've told you all, separately, how Eve did, and how the embryo did. I just wanted to pop back in while you're all together to see if you have any questions. Eve?"

"When do I go home?"

"Ah. Perhaps Sunday. Let's see how you do this afternoon. Hopefully, we'll be able to get you into your room soon."

"Also, I feel a little drunk." I looked at my parents and added, "Not that I'd know what that feels like."

"It's just the anesthesia, Eve," said the doctor. "It'll wear off over the next few hours."

"Perfect! I think." Then I thought of something else. "The other thing I was wondering about.... Well, could you tell us a little bit about our itty-bitty embryo?"

She smiled and kept her eyes on me. "The procedure went extremely well for the embryo. When I got in, I found a perfect sac with an appropriately sized embryo."

I said, authoritatively, "Half-way between a medium green olive and a prune."

"Exactly," said Dr. Hughey, nodding to me. "With clear visualization and access, it was a simple matter to examine, extract and photograph the embryo, and get it into the preservation canister. Then, I stitched you up. Degradable stitches inside, and removable ones along the bikini line. Now, you just need to rest."

"That's all I have to do? Cool."

"Well, the nurses will have you draw air out of the spirometer, which may hurt a little. But it will keep you from getting fluid in your lungs. And they'll probably have you walking shortly after we get you into a room."

"And just to double-check, you do really think our teeny-tiny embryo will do fine in the future?"

"Yes, Eve. I believe the embryo will transplant and resume its growth well. What's so exciting about this for me is that it's the very first embryo to have been retrieved this way." She smiled and added, "I should tell you that it would give this experiment the very best chance for success if the uterus into which it's transferred is yours."

"Whose else would it be?" I think I said that real defensively—like she'd insulted me.

Dr. Hughey said, "I told you that you and Adam are also free to donate it to an infertile couple, should your circumstances dictate that it doesn't work out for you to resume the pregnancy. Remember?"

"Yes," I said. "I do...now that you mention it." I smiled at her so she'd know I forgave her for the insult.

"It's a decision for you and Adam to make. There's no hurry. It can be done any time in the next twenty-five years."

I looked at Adam and said, "Do you think that'll be enough time for us to decide?"

He laughed. "Yes, Eve. Enough time." He turned to the doctor lady, and said, "But it really should be Eve?"

"Yes, Adam. As you can imagine, she would be the very best host."

"Hostess," I said, for no good reason and then laughed.

Dr. Hughey smiled and went on, "As we discussed, you would take hormones to prepare yourself, and then we would do the procedure."

"Surgery?" asked Dad.

"Possibly. But I may be able to manage it vaginally," she said. She clapped her hands together and smiled broadly at all of us. "Anyway, all of this is for another day—and I definitely plan to review all of this with you, Eve, when you're not in recovery."

I winked at her and said, "I'm picking up what you're putting down." Then I had another worry. I interrupted her and tried to put it the best way I could. "Since it could be like a quarter century from now, who'd do it for me if you're…not practicing by then?"

She laughed. "It's a good question. If I'm unavailable—shall we say—the other doctors in my practice will be trained to carry on."

"Oh, good." I smiled at her again.

She said, "I just wanted to meet with you all to be sure I've answered any questions. Mr. and Mrs. Gehraghty, I'll be back to see Eve on Sunday morning. Then we'll decide whether I can discharge her." She turned to me. "Any other questions, Eve?"

"Nope. Good to go! Wait. Where am I going again?"

"Your room, Eve." The doctor patted my hand. "Well, feel free to call me or email me any time if any questions should come to you."

I took this as a very sincere invitation. I said, "Thanks, I'll do it!"

She turned to my parents and Adam. "Mr. and Mrs. Gehraghty? Adam? Is there anything I haven't addressed?"

Mom said, "I think I'm fine for now, doctor." Then, turning to my dad, "Dan?"

"No questions at the moment. We'll contact you if anything comes up."

"Please do." She looked at Adam. "Questions?"

"I'm sure I will have some. May I just email you, as well?"

"Absolutely. I encourage it, Adam." She looked at each

one of us and then smiled and said, "Then I guess I'll be on my way."

"Thanks, doctor." I said. "I'm very happy. And grateful." My eyes started to tear up. "We just saved our itty-bitty little embryo's life."

Dr. Hughey nodded and said, "You should be very proud. You've taken an important step forward for science—when you didn't have to."

I sniffled. "Actually, doctor, I did have to. It was the only way to end being pregnant and save the embryo too." I smiled at Dr. Hughey, my parents, and Adam, tears now running down my cheeks.

Dr. Hughey nodded. Then she walked up to me and reached out her arm to shake my hand. "You're an unusual young woman, Eve. I'm proud to know you." With that, she left the room.

I was embarrassed because I definitely wasn't looking for praise. Wasn't what I'd just said the whole point of everything the doctor and I did? Well, I was glad she was so happy about it too. Fortunately, my parents could tell I didn't like the compliment, and didn't follow up on how unusual I am. A nurse knocked on the door, then entered with my lunch tray.

Mom said, "Adam, if you'd like to visit with Eve for a while, Dan and I will dash downstairs for some yummy cafeteria food. My stomach's starting to remind me that we all skipped breakfast."

"I would love to stay with Eve. Thank you," said Adam.

Dad offered to bring back a sandwich for Adam, and they left.

"I like Dr. Hughey," said Adam.

"I know. Isn't she great?"

"Yes. So enthusiastic…and honest. I also feel she is a very kind woman."

I laughed out loud. "Of course. She's Canadian."

Adam sat by my bed as I ate the cheese sandwich and cup of tomato soup I'd been served. Once my tray had been removed, he asked me if I had any pain yet.

"Not much. But the doctor lady promised it, Adam. I can tell you now I'm not taking any pain medicines and get hooked and become a heroin addict. Not me!" I smiled.

"Maybe just take it an hour at a time. I'll be here with you."

"Great! How long can you stay?"

"I will be here as long as you are in the hospital. So, sometime on Sunday, whenever you leave for home. I just have to let Gerhard's mother know when I'd like to fly again…to climb into this ridiculous suit again." He laughed.

"Do you have any other clothes with you?"

"Of course. I am well-outfitted. I have three purple t-shirts and two pairs of cargo shorts. Oh, and gym shoes."

"Have you got a coat?"

"Actually, we forgot about the weather difference. So, no. In fact, I am not sure that Vincent Garcia owns a winter coat."

"Why would he?" I laughed.

"Right. So, tomorrow I will just jog over here to keep warm."

"Adam, you'll look silly in shorts and a t-shirt."

"Ah, but you see, I will look silly either way. I am just so happy you are okay, and our embryo did well."

"Me, too."

A nurse came by and looked at screens and records and me. Then she told us I'd be moved shortly into a regular room. Within fifteen minutes, she and a male nurse swooped in and wheeled me down the hall, up a floor in an elevator, and into a room. Adam stayed with me the whole time. I was happy to see they'd parked me in a single—mainly because I craved privacy any time I could be alone with him. There was a green, vinyl recliner in a corner by a small window. A pillow and blanket were sitting on it. The nurse explained they were for any over-night visitor. There were also two smaller chairs, so no one had to sit on the corner of my bed once my parents got back from their lunch.

Once I was settled in my room, I was allowed to get up to walk to my bathroom. A nurse carried my embarrassing urine bag and pulled the coat tree holding my IV stuff behind us like an awkward shadow. As soon as I got back in bed, I hit a wall and suddenly felt completely exhausted. I told Adam I needed a little nap and asked if he'd hold my hand.

"Of course I will."

I felt the warmth of his fingers encircling mine, closed my eyes, and immediately drifted off. I suppose it was all the stress--and the fact I hadn't slept a wink the night before. Ap-parently, I was out for most of the day because when I woke up suddenly, it was dark outside. Adam was still holding my hand. I asked him if that hadn't been uncomfortable for him for such a long time. He smiled his tender smile. "Eve, I have been in heaven, sitting by your side, watching you sleep."

"Well, now I wish I'd stayed awake to watch you watching me. But that wouldn't have worked, would it?"

"No."

My head felt back to normal, and I wasn't sure exactly what any of us had said right after the operation. I thought I remembered it all—but I couldn't swear to it. "So, where are my parents?"

"You mean your 'rents?"

"What?"

He laughed. "They left for the cafeteria for dinner about thirty minutes ago. We have all been sitting here quietly. They have been doing work."

"Yeah. They do that."

"But only because you were asleep. Also, they feared that you would wake while they are at dinner."

"Oh, I'm sure. It's like them to worry about me."

"Your parents are wonderful, Eve."

"Yeah. They really are." I suddenly remembered my promise to call Claire after the procedure, and asked Adam if it would be okay for me to have privacy to call her.

"Of course. You must talk with your friend. She has probably been very worried." He kissed my cheek, and then walked toward the door. "Eve, I will just wander the halls. I won't go far in case you need me. Do you have an idea how much time I should be absent?"

"Maybe ten minutes," I said. Then I added, "Maximum," and smiled.

"Very good. I will just peek in to see if you have finished your call at that time."

"Thanks, Adam."

I rang Claire's cell number. "Hi, Claire. It's me."

"Oh my God! Eve. I've been waiting for your call. That was a heck of a long surgery! How are you?"

"Fine. I'm okay. Sorry. I fell asleep after. But I'm okay. And Dr. Hughey said the embryo did well, which was a huge relief."

"I guess so. Since that was the whole point. So, you're really okay?"

"Yeah, Claire. I'm really fine."

"Oh, good. I'm so relieved. Aren't you thrilled to have the surgery behind you?"

"No kidding. I didn't even get gorked by the anesthesia, like in some of my mom's cases. I swear, Claire, one time this perfectly normal woman became a vegetable because she got too much of it."

"Well, you could afford to lose a few IQ points—but not all of them."

"Exactly. I mean, who could?"

"Are you feeling any better about Adam?"

"Oh yeah. He just stepped out into the hall so I could have some privacy to call you."

"What?"

"I know! Claire, he came all the way from the DR to be with me."

"But how? I thought he didn't have any money. And I thought he was pissed at you for not telling him sooner."

"First of all, he doesn't have any money. But his friend's mom got him a buddy pass for his round trip. It's actually a funny story. I'll tell you when I get home. Second, he's forgiven me, and thinks he was unfair to me, too. So he apologized for that."

"Cool. But why?"

"He said he was wrong not to have looked at it from

my point of view. And when he did, he was able to see why I wanted to have the surgery."

"Wow."

"Yeah. Adam's a very thoughtful person." I was fiddling with a magazine Mom had brought for me, flipping pages mindlessly.

"I'm sure he is."

"I said that badly. I don't mean 'thoughtful' as in, kind to others. Although he's that, too. I mean he really thinks things through. We've both been working on changing our focus, to look at things from the other person's point of view. It's not natural, you know. You really have to work at it."

"Honestly, Eve, I never really tried to do it before you started talking about it so much. And it is hard."

"Hm."

"Anyway, did your folks meet Adam?"

"Oh, yeah."

"And?"

"At first, Dad was stand-offish. But he got to know Adam a little, and now he seems to really like him. Mom liked him from the moment they met."

"That's amazing. Here this guy knocks up their daughter on a church service trip, and they're fine with it."

"I wouldn't put it like that. More like, they'd already accepted the fact I was pregnant. So they were open to meet Adam as a person, rather than just the impregnator."

"How does he feel about them?"

"He says he thinks they're great. I'll tell you, it's a huge load off my mind that Adam's not mad at me, and that he and my parents get along so well. If I didn't have this slice in my belly like Frankenstein's monster, everything would be great."

"Where's the slice?"

"Oh, you know—like a C-section. It's horizontal just under the top edge of my bikini line. So no one will ever see it if I dress remotely modestly."

"That is a shame. Since I know how much you've dreamed of a career as a nude dancer."

"True."

"Do you have much pain?"

"Not yet. Thank God. Although Dr. Hughey told me it's usually worse the day after." I was tired of fooling with the magazine and tried to toss it on the green chair. It fell, splayed out on the floor. After that, I only had the phone cord to play with as we talked.

"Well, I hope it's not too bad." She paused. "I've been thinking about you, Eve."

"Thanks."

"Actually, what I mean is that I've been trying to look at this thing from the embryo's point of view—like you've been saying."

"And?"

"And, I can see why you think it has a right to its future--it's just on its track, like all of us. And that it'll be a regular person in a few months, unless someone deliberately derails it. I get how that can be true at the same time it's absolutely true a woman has the right not to have to stay pregnant. Frankly, it took me a while to let myself see it."

"I know. It was hard for me to get my head around it, too. Especially the way we're all trained to focus on how right we are. It's like everyone thinks she has to choose a side, and then fight like a crazy person for it."

"But here's the thing. Even though I can see what you're saying, we're just not there yet, Eve."

"Of course we're not."

"Right. So, until most unwanted pregnancies can be prevented, and until the ones that aren't can be solved by the freezing thing, well, we have no choice but to keep picking sides. And even though I totally admit the embryo's getting a bad deal, I have to go with the woman's side."

"Me, too."

"What do you mean, 'me, too'? I thought you'd become anti-abortion unless the embryo can be frozen."

"No. That was just my solution, for me."

"So, you don't believe that?"

"I might've been thinking like that. But now I see it's not that simple. The truth is, I don't see many women wanting to go through what I just did. Maybe some would want to do the procedure with just the catheter. But, shit, this is no solution, Claire."

"Well, what do you believe…now?"

"I think we need to go with your futuristic idea. We need to work together to so we can have birth control from puberty—like you said, for all girls. But you're right. We're not there yet. And until we are, we have to keep abortions legal."

"Well, any time you agree with me, I know you're on the right track. But what's made you choose the woman over the embryo?"

"It's pretty obvious, isn't it? I mean, there's really no choice to make. If *Roe* were overturned now, women would still get abortions. It would just be more dangerous, especially for poor women--which solves absolutely nothing."

"What about what you said before, that the embryo has a right to its future?"

"Oh, I still believe that."

"I don't get it. Whose side are you on?"

"Your question's the problem, Claire. It shouldn't be about 'sides.' There are legit reasons both sides are right. But they're based on what's moral, not what's legal. It's like if a married person has an affair. It's immoral, but you don't go to jail for it."

"Maybe. But let me ask you this, Eve. If Dr. Hughey didn't exist, what would you've done?"

I paused to think and shook my head to myself. "I don't know."

"You're shitting me. After all you've been through, you still don't know?"

"That's right. Some women may be so sure about it, one way or the other, it wouldn't even be a question. But I suspect there are lots more like me, who really don't know until they're forced to decide."

"That's tough."

"No shit. But there is a solution—your solution. Obviously, we can't fix it overnight. But we can get to where we need to be, in time. Damn it—we need resources. And we need scientists to push hard. But, the way I see it, the main thing we women need to do is to quit fighting about it and work together."

"Sorry to have to say this, but it'll never happen."

"Never's a long time, Claire. I know a lot of older folks have hardening of the arteries around it. But, somehow, somebody has to get through to young women."

"But how?"

"We do it! Any way we can think of. I have one idea for something I can do right away."

"Cool. What?"

"Dr. Hughey. Adam and I should give her permission to go ahead with an article she wants to write about my procedure."

"Hm."

"Of course, she'd use pseudonyms for me and Adam. But she warned me someone might figure out it was me. Not so much a risk for Adam, since almost nobody even knows he went to Toronto."

"But how the heck could anyone know it's about you?"

"Well, let's say Dr. Hughey's article makes a big splash and spreads beyond the medical journal. Let's say it makes the news on CNN or goes viral or something. And, you know, it's just the kind of thing that would."

"True."

"Remember how school will have a doctor's note about my laparotomy from an ob/gyn in Toronto. That's already a little odd…a little attention-getting, wouldn't you say?"

"Yeah, I'd say so."

"So, what if Ms. Griffin or someone else makes the connection? Which wouldn't be too hard. I mean, how many Dr. Mary Hugheys from Toronto could there be? It could still be fine, except for the grapevine thing. It could totally get around. And if it did, this would be even worse than me being pregnant in school."

"Yeah, Eve. It would definitely spread like wildfire. But

why do you think it'd be worse?"

"Because lots of people would think what I did is really weird."

"That could be. Since it is. So, what do you want to do?"

"Well, Dr. Hughey won't let us decide about the article until two weeks from now."

"That's nice. Not while your brain's still addled by anesthesia or pain."

"Exactly. So, this time everybody will be in on it—Mom, Dad, Adam and me. Right now, I'd say we tell her to publish and don't worry about ourselves…myself. How else can we get people talking about it?"

"I have a crazy idea, Eve. But you're gonna hate it."

"I don't hate it. I already thought of it. After Dr. Hughey's article comes out, I write an essay on why I went through it."

"Yes! Brilliant minds…. But maybe wait to see if Dr. Hughey gets death threats and shit."

"I know. Some nut-ball might even try to do something violent."

"Do you think Dr. Hughey worries about it?"

"I doubt it. Since she did publish the article two years ago about the two embryos that were done with the catheter. I didn't think to ask her about death threats—but I will before we make our decision."

"But what if she did get them, Eve? What if she expects more?"

"I'm really not afraid of ignorant people. My parents would say it's because I'm young and still feel invincible. But I need them to agree before I'd say yes to Dr. Hughey's article or write my own essay. I sure don't want to get their house t-peed or firebombed or something."

"Good point."

"But, honestly, I think they'll support both. You know, they've been trying to get me more interested in service since I was a little girl. This would be service. And I'm ready to do it. In fact, I think I'd really disappoint myself if I didn't jump on this. I've come to see that scientists can't just sit back on our bar stools looking through microscopes."

"You mean future scientists."

"Of course. We have to stand up for what's right, just like anybody else."

"Even at the risk of throwing yourself into high school hell?"

"Yeah. Some things are more important than a hell-free senior year."

"I can't disagree with that. I think. But just a suggestion, Eve. When you do go off to college, make friends with the security guards. You may need them."

"Brilliant. I'll bake cookies for them." I laughed. "Crap!"

"What 'crap'?"

"I just remembered. I sent Adam out to wander the halls. I've really gotta go, Claire. I'm glad we talked. Come by Sunday night for the viewing of the scar."

"Are you kidding? I wouldn't miss it."

Adam peeked his head in the door, and I waved him in. "Bye, Claire!"

"Good visit?" said Adam.

"Great visit. Thanks for the privacy."

A few minutes later Mom and Dad walked back into the room. "You're awake! How do you feel?" asked Mom.

"Around the incision feels really tight. But I just have a little bit of pain. I really feel fine."

"Oh, good," said Dad. "Your mother and I were talking over our meal. And we'd like to offer Adam the opportunity to stay with you tonight, if that's what you two would like."

"Thanks so much!" I said. I knew Dad was trying to give me a gift. And he was willing to overlook the fact that it would also be a gift to Adam. After all, what trouble could the two of us get into at this point?

"Yes," added Mom, "only one visitor is allowed overnight. And we just thought, since Adam will be leaving on Sunday, this might suit you."

"Nothing would make me happier, Mrs. Gehraghty. Thank you both for the offer."

"We have another idea, too," said Dad. "We want to see you in the morning, Eve. So, we'll be here when visiting hours start at 10:00 a.m. But we had the thought that you two would probably enjoy some privacy on your one full day together...."

"We would," I said and smiled at him.

"So, your mother and I will play tourist the rest of the day and come back after dinner tomorrow."

"Wait! You're not just going to a library and pull out your laptops, are you?" I asked.

"No," said Mom. "We do too much of that. We're going to be real tourists."

"That's great, guys! You definitely should go on more dates," I said.

"Wonderful. Then it's a plan," said Mom.

Chapter 21

Adam and I talked for another couple of hours after they left. Adam made up the lounge chair to sleep beside me. I became drowsy again and fell back into a deep sleep. Of course, I was interrupted several times during the night by nurses walking in and switching on the overhead fluorescent light to take my temperature, or blood pressure, or give me a dose of Tylenol. For the most part, when I woke, I saw Adam sleeping soundly. Watching him sleep gave me the most incredible sense of well-being. Just having him with me produced a kind of euphoria. This was in spite of the fact that the pain had arrived with a vengeance. I tried hard not to focus on the feeling I was being stabbed in the stomach.

I needed to practice ignoring the pain because I definitely didn't want my one full day with Adam to be ruined by my constant moaning and groaning. I planned to use Adam's face as my *anchor of concentration*, a trick I'd learned when my folks dragged me to a series of mindfulness meditation classes. I also knew leaving him on Sunday would be almost unbearable, so I needed to block that out of my mind, too. My plan was to refuse to let either of those problems mess up the incredible luxury of having Adam all to myself in the morning. Frankly, I was pretty sure I didn't have the discipline to pull it off. But at least I knew what my goal was.

The nurses' station was just outside my door, which was usually closed, keeping all their noise out pretty well. But one of the night nurses left the door open as she left. The nurses sitting out there had to have seen my door was open. They probably assumed I was asleep since it was the middle of the night. I heard one of them say my name which, of course, perked up my ears.

"No. I'm talking about Eve Geraghty. You won't believe this, but her boyfriend's name is Adam."

"Ha. What're the chances?" came a man's voice in response. "He seems pleasant enough. Odd fashion sense though." I smiled.

The woman spoke again. "I'm shocked her parents let her have this Dr. Hughey special. She just seems so young to have an unnecessary laparotomy. I wonder if she got any say in it?"

"Are you kidding?" replied the man. "This thing got her off the hook. So, I'm thinking Miss Eve was completely on board."

"Maybe." A call button sounded and the woman abruptly added, "Gotta go."

After that, I listened carefully, but my name didn't come up again. It stuck with me. "Got her off the hook." My first thought was that the male nurse must not be Canadian. Of course, I knew the reputation for kindness was a gross generalization. I suppose I'd held onto it because it's just so sweet. But, unkind or not, the male nurse's statement bothered me more because I'd overheard it. I always thought stuff like that was extra valid because people were saying things they really believed but wouldn't say to my face. I already felt embarrassed by my privilege. Not just about Dad's credit card. There was also the fact I hadn't had to miss my first Toronto appointment because Mom had a wealthy friend who happened to own a jet. And I was lucky Mom and Dad were able to check Dr. Hughey's credentials with people who were in the know. All of which had led to my not being pregnant anymore, and not having aborted my embryo. What the nurse had said made me sound like a spoiled child. Maybe I was.

But I didn't think so. I didn't think guiding your young adult kid was the same thing as spoiling her. When my parents gave me the book-reading assignment, I took it as seriously as an unwanted pregnancy. I did my reading and my thinking and I came up with a conclusion and an idea. Was I lucky Dr. Hughey had time to work with me? Of course. Did I get a break that my parents could provide the moral support and resources to follow through on my idea? Absolutely. But the truth is, I'm the one who came up with the solution. I'm the one who pestered Joel to loan us his Cessna. I'm the one who decided to have a major surgery, rather than a quick abortion. I decided to do all of it for the embryo. And yet, there I was, sitting in a hospital bed with serious abdominal pain, expecting six weeks of discomfort, and no soccer after that, being insulted by a man who knew nothing about me—who'd never had an unwanted pregnancy.

The more I thought about the unfairness of his comment, the more upset I got. I went from embarrassed to enraged in just a few minutes. I'm sure my blood pressure was going up. Thankfully, my monitor didn't beep. Eventually it came to me that his lack of knowledge was the whole answer. He didn't know any of my history. And he didn't know anything about being a woman. I couldn't figure out whether his ignorance was his own fault or not. But his phrase stayed with me--"off the hook." Why, exactly, was the woman the one in the couple who was "on the hook" in the first place? Why was the woman the one to feel ill one week out of every month from the time she's twelve or thirteen years old? Why was the woman the one to be branded after two people had consensual sex, the result showing up only on her? Why has science and technology taken us to a place where we can talk to a friend in China, face-to-face, in an instant, or share close-up pictures of Mars, but we can't prevent unwanted pregnancies?

It boggled my mind that the best science has to offer women is a Midol and a handful of imperfect birth control devices, all of which, except the condom, must be bought and used by the woman. Why is there no research on Claire's idea of delaying periods until a woman wants to get pregnant? Or at least, beginning birth control for all girls at puberty? And why aren't women excited about work like Dr. Hughey's? This is just messed up. And the phrase "off the hook" will likely always raise my blood pressure. In fact, I'll probably never want to go fishing again, to avoid it coming up! I didn't wake Adam to tell him how the male nurse's comment brought me to a middle-of-the-night rant in my head. I just tried to calm myself down so I could get some sleep.

On Saturday morning, the pain was even worse. It was the least terrible when I sat still, but when I had to exhale enough air to do my spirometer exercises, I was in agony. It was like I was being stabbed from the outside and the inside at the same time. It had only helped a little that the pinch-machine urine catheter had been removed. I kept saying no to the pain meds because I was so afraid of becoming an addict. When the nurses got me up to walk, my body made it clear I didn't really want to stand up straight. I walked leaning over, like an old, arthritic woman. Telling Adam half-truths hadn't gone well, so I shared with him exactly how I felt. One time when I was doing a tough exhale into the tube, my eyes actually teared up from the pain. Adam bent over me to wipe my cheeks, and I saw that his eyes were also clouded --as though pain were contagious.

But most of our hours together were great, in spite of the pain. As promised, Mom and Dad stopped by for about a half hour, just as visiting hours were starting. I didn't tell them the expected horror had begun. After what their marriage had been through because of me, there was no way I'd put a damper on their date. I could see it was a beautiful sunny day, and I verbally shoved them out the door to get going with their tourist adventure.

Adam and I spent the day talking and laughing. I did tell him, second only to the spirometer, laughing was what hurt the most. Nevertheless, laughing until it hurt just made me laugh more. I must've tormented myself with the laughter/pain combo for hours. I was determined not to take anything stronger than extra-strength Tylenol, which, as far as I could tell, was about as helpful as popping a Pez. It surprised me, but using Adam's beautiful face as my *anchor of concentration* really did seem to help a lot. We talked about his town and mine, his gymnasium and my high school, our childhoods, our best friends Claire and Gerhard, and his darling brothers.

But one exchange had gone very badly. It was my own fault. Adam said, "From what Dr. Hughey said, it seems it would be best if the embryo were to be brought into the world through you—assuming whomever you're with at the time doesn't insist you donate it." He paused, then kind of stammered. "I can understand your partner might not want his baby to be another man's offspring. And, in that case, I'd probably agree we should donate it."

I knew all of that was possible. Probably even likely. But

it crushed me like an elephant had just decided to sit on my chest. I knew I had no right to be angry with Adam. But it felt like rejection. I didn't say anything until he sensed the change of temperature in the room and insisted I tell him what was bothering me. It was extremely embarrassing to admit the truth, but I was finally able to spit it out. "Adam, what you said sounds like you're dumping me."

He looked at me as though I'd just slapped him. "How could you think that, Eve? Seriously, do you have no faith in me?" He left the room and closed the door softly behind him. I didn't think anything while he was gone. I was numb. But when he returned, he apologized. He said something like, "Eve, I love you. I would never hurt you. You just had major surgery to save our embryo." He looked at the ceiling for a few moments, as though something important was written up there. I felt a panic at what he might say next. Then he held my hand and looked into my eyes. "I have been afraid to admit how deeply I feel for you, Eve. That thing I said was meant to relieve you from pressure if you meet someone else. It was not about me dumping you. It was about you dumping me. I was trying to give you a gift of permission. For in the future…when it might have value to you." He apologized again.

Of course, I started crying uncontrollably. Once I'd finally calmed down, I told him I was the one who should apologize. I just wasn't ready to go into all of the possible scenarios. I'd overreacted. And this whole thing was going to be freaking hard. But on that day, together in person, I just couldn't talk about all of that. He nodded and then leaned over to kiss me. We resumed our stories about our lives. My overreaction was left behind us. The truth was, we were interrupted so often by the nurses that, by the end of the day, we had to agree it hadn't been an ideal venue for a date. But we'd gotten to know each other a little better, and I loved him even more.

My parents returned around 7:30 that evening and were giddy with all they'd seen and done. I'd never seen them so obviously thrilled with each other's company. I suppose almost ruining your marriage over a disagreement and then finding a solution must've been a powerful aphrodisiac. I say this only because they seemed not only happy, but obviously in love. I assumed Mom had apologized for what she'd threatened. The truth is, either way I'd gone with my decision, our family would've made it work. It would've been hard. But we would've gotten through it. I'd come to understand that going forward with the Retrieval and Preservation hadn't been needed to save my family. It had been needed to save me.

Mom had sneaked some shopping bags into the room, and I assumed she'd gotten a get-well gift for me. In a way, she had. After we'd all talked for a while about our day and their day, she reached for the two bags and handed them to Adam. He looked surprised and said, "Shall I open these for Eve?"

Mom replied, "No. You should open them for you."

He looked at me, and I said, "Go ahead. I'm dying to see what my folks got for you."

Adam looked into the first bag and then laughed hard. "I can see you were only humoring me when you said my tan suit looked just fine." He pulled out a navy sport coat, grey slacks, white shirt, navy and light blue striped tie, and a pair of black loafers. "Mr. and Mrs. Geraghty, it is all beautiful. But you really should not have...."

"It's nothing," interrupted Mom. "Anyway, we got everything on sale." She and Dad were smiling at him.

"How did you know the sizes, Mom?"

"I'm observant."

I persisted, "Okay. But what about the shoe size?"

"Oh, I peeked at the high heeled ones when we stopped by this morning." She shrugged. "They were just sitting by Adam's chair." I shook my head and laughed.

"But this is too generous," said Adam.

Dad spoke up, which was encouraging. But he seemed really serious. "Listen, Adam. No matter what happens between you and Eve, whether you stay together, whether you become just good friends or part ways, it'll always be true that you're the father of our daughter's Toronto embryo. So, we certainly don't want you going around looking like a goofball." He laughed, and then we all did. I was thrilled to see Dad had warmed to Adam. My parents didn't stay long. They knew this was my last night with him for a long time. Maybe forever.

After they left, Adam said, "I feel I have to tell you I'm very embarrassed at such a gift. But I feared I would hurt their feelings to decline it."

"I'm sorry. It was kinda over the top. They do that sometimes. Of course, it wasn't really about the clothes--they were saying they accept you and they like you. So, you're right, Adam. It would've hurt their feelings if you'd said 'no thanks.'"

Adam responded by saying that he still couldn't get over how my parents were so accepting of him. Especially when he was the one who had caused all the problems in the first place.

I reminded him that "he" had caused nothing. "We" had caused the situation. And even if I'd known then what I know now, I wouldn't have done a thing differently. A lot had happened, for sure. And some of it had been incredibly painful. But I'd learned so much about myself, and my parents, and Adam. And about relationships—which I'd be more careful with in the future. Although I didn't mention it, I also thought my parents would be more careful with theirs. I told Adam that I thought people really have to invest in dating, like any friendship we care about. I knew I was sounding pretty corny.

Adam said, "So, then should we talk about where our relationship might go?"

"I suppose so. I mean, we can't just pretend we'll be together, like we've been for the past two days. It's tough to face it though."

"I know, Eve. But I think we must be realistic."

"Of course. 'Realistic' says we write old-fashioned snail-mail letters until August. Then, once you're home in Germany, we can text, Instagram, Face Time…. Whatever we can think of."

"Yes. That will be better."

"And then what?"

"Well, in four years, if I can get a scholarship to medical school in the United States, it will be easier to see you. The added benefit is the incentive I will have to excel in my studies to ensure this."

"It would be heaven to have you in the States." I smiled because I'd thought of another way we could see each other. I said, "And in the meantime, what about working together at the orphanage in the summers?" It hit me that was something I could look forward to that might keep me going.

"I'm sorry to have to say this, Eve, but in truth, I can only work there if I get one of the paid counselor-level positions."

"I'll bet you could. And if you do, I'll definitely come down as a volunteer." I hesitated and added, "But, honestly, it would break my heart to be there without you."

"I know. I feel that now."

I had another exciting idea. "So maybe I could do my junior year abroad in Germany…near where you will be at university."

"That would be incredible, Eve. How I would love to show you around my country."

As we discussed all the possibilities, I began to feel hopeful about our future. I don't think I was blind to the realities of a long-distance relationship. But I was beginning to see it might actually be possible. There was no point agonizing over it. We would both do our best over miles and years. The odds were definitely against us. The weight of my longing for Adam could easily drag me down. Much was really up to me—how maturely I could handle it. But a lot was also out of my control. There was only one thing to do—take it a day at a time and do my best. Easy to say, anyway.

Chapter 22

On Sunday morning, Adam walked back to the hostel to shower and shave. When he returned to the hospital wearing the things my folks had bought for him, he looked like a young businessman. The tan suit had definitely not been his best look. It was like he was growing more handsome each day he spent in Toronto. To someone else, he probably just looked like a completely different handsome young man. But to me, he looked like my destiny.

Adam leaned in to kiss me and then pulled up one of the small chairs to sit close to me. "How are you feeling?"

"Mentally or physically?"

"Let's start with physically."

"I'm good. Just some horrible pain in my stomach when I do anything. And I walk like a hunchback since my body keeps telling me good posture's not all it's cracked up to be. Oh, and Dr. Hughey's already stopped by to examine me. She said she'd order the discharge. So, I must be at the right place on my slow path to recovery."

"When can you leave here?"

"She said it could take up to a couple of hours for everything. A nurse will come by at some point with my discharge instructions."

"Wonderful. And how are you feeling mentally?"

"I'm working hard at being mature about this. So far, so good. Although I suspect I could fall apart at any moment."

"I love you, Eve."

"I love you, too. It's lucky we're both such mature types, or we could both melt down into pools of tears."

"Yes. It is very lucky." Adam walked to the window and

stood there looking out without speaking for a minute or so. Then he turned to me, smiled and said, "Have your parents booked your flight home?"

"Mom's doing it now, down in the lounge. They'd like to get home as soon as possible, so I assume it'll be early afternoon. Should you call Gerhard's mother about your flight?"

"Yes. I will. I would just like to visit with you until your mother returns. I would prefer to take a flight after yours."

"Why?"

"I suppose I will feel less like I'm deserting you."

I smiled and said, "I understand." Then I added, "Maybe we could share a cab back to the airport."

"That would be nice."

The time up until my discharge was busy. Nurses were monitoring things and measuring things and making notes like mad. Sadly, they gave me the spirometer to take home and told me to use the thing for three more days. Mom, Dad, and Adam were all with me, but the atmosphere was so chaotic that private conversation was impossible. They took turns running back to their hotels to pick up their luggage so we'd all be ready to head to the airport at the same time.

Everything was set for my discharge at noon. Mom had booked a 4:00 p.m. flight home for us, and Adam's was scheduled for 5:30 p.m. We were assigned to different terminals, so as it turned out, Adam needed to jump out of the cab first. We all stepped out to say our goodbyes at Adam's terminal. Mom and Dad both hugged him. He approached me last, hugged me very tenderly, and kissed me softly. The tearing eyes thing proved to be contagious again--mine reflected in Adam's, and then in my parents'. Like on my last night at the orphanage, it felt as though someone was ripping stubborn Velcro to separate us. He stopped at the glass door into the terminal and waved to us one last time.

Back in our cab, walking through the lines at security and customs in Toronto slowly and stooped like an old lady, waiting for and sitting through our flight, and then on the way home by cab, I paid no attention to anything around me. I have no memories at all of the details of the trip home. It was like I'd been semi-conscious. Tears escaped pretty often, so it was lucky Mom had gotten me a couple of packs of tissues at the airport. She must've known I'd be super-emotional. The whole time, I thought of nothing but Adam.

Once we got home, I went up to my room to get some rest before Claire was scheduled to come over for the *viewing of the scar*. I'd only been gone four days. But everything looked different. It was like new eyes had been implanted as a part of my surgery. All the tangible things I had--our comfortable house, my retro bedroom, and my closet full of clothes—all of it felt insignificant. But the presence of my parents in my life, and Claire and, of course, Adam, felt incredibly important.

As I lay back on my bed, I felt a sharp pain but it wasn't abdominal. It was my heart. Then a lump showed up in my throat and just stayed there. I assumed I was in the early stages of grief over losing Adam. There was no doubt we'd keep in touch as we'd talked about at the hospital. But his physical presence was what I needed. And it was something I just couldn't have. Maybe, ever. My eyes welled up and the lump in my throat turned into gasps for air. I knew what to do if I started hyperventilating, which seemed a distinct possibility. I let myself cry until my eyes ran dry. I thought it would take years for my heart to heal, if healing were even possible. I tried to calm myself with breathing exercises and eventually nodded off. When I awoke, nothing had changed, and I felt even sadder.

Mom called up to me that she'd talked with Claire, who'd be over in fifteen minutes. I knew she'd give me shit for wallowing and I needed her to. I also realized I'd need to rely a lot on Claire to get through this. Her little insights, stupid jokes and just her presence would be like life preservers she'd toss out to me. She wouldn't let me sink.

It's funny how brave and self-sufficient I'd felt during many moments over those four days in Toronto. But back at home, I saw I was totally dependent on the people I loved to keep me moving forward. I hoped my grief would eventually give way to something less painful--maybe more of a dull ache. At that point, I was having a really hard time thinking positively. I saw no reason for optimism. When Claire walked into my room, I tried to smile at her, but it turned into sobs.

"Oh, my God. Eve, what's going on?"

"Nothing," I managed to say through my crying.

She sat by me on the bed and handed me the box of tissues from my dresser. "Don't try to say anything. There's nothing wrong with a good cry. I'll be here when you feel like talking."

I just nodded and tried to get a grip. I pointed to a glass of water on the other night stand and Claire brought it to me, then sat right next to me on the bed. I swallowed a few gulps and then took a very deep breath to calm myself. That caused me to cry out. Focusing only on Adam, I'd forgotten how sore my stomach muscles were.

"That must've hurt."

"A little. Anyway, I'm sorry about being such a baby."

"Is it about the embryo or Adam?"

"Adam."

"I get it. After having him with you in Toronto, you love him even more, and now he's gone."

I pressed my palms against my eyes to keep from starting up again. "Yeah. Claire, I had no idea it would hurt so much. It's like he's died."

Claire pushed my hair back out of my face where it had gotten stuck in the tears. "But he hasn't."

"I know. But he may as well have. It's only February. And I can't do anything but write snail mail letters to him until August."

"But you *can* write letters to him. They say it's a lost art, you know. So, do it. Write great letters. Learn more about him and let him learn more about you."

"What?"

"I just mean it's a great chance to see if you like how he thinks, if his ideas are interesting to you. And vice versa. Maybe you'll find out whether he's really the boy worth keeping up with and planning around. When he's with you, his hotness gets in the way and distracts you from that other stuff."

I squinted at her. "Claire, why are you acting so freaking mature about this? I don't get it." She smiled at me so knowingly and patiently that I knew something special was behind it.

"You know, we buried Grandma Sally on January 2nd. It really hit me hard."

"Oh, my God. I'm so sorry, Claire. I didn't even ask how you're doing."

"It's okay." She looked so sad and I assumed part of it was because she was disappointed in me. "It's just that I was too little to remember when my grandpa died, so my reaction surprised me."

"How do you feel?"

"As sad as I felt the day she died. You know how close we were."

"Yeah. I do."

"So, it's the finality that's killing me. It's crazy. I never would've been visiting with her during weekdays because I was always in school. But now I miss her all the time, especially when I'm in school. And I finally figured out what it is."

"What?" I bit my lip and felt a flush of embarrassment that I hadn't remembered her loss.

"It's that there's no future with her. It used to be that I really looked forward to seeing her when I got home from school. It's not just that I can't see her anymore. It's also that I can't look forward to a time when I will be able to see her."

"I'm so sorry. She was such a sweet lady."

"And funny. Super witty. And interesting. God, Eve, I had so much fun with her."

"I know."

"That's why I think you'll be able to come out of your funk over Adam. He's still alive. And probably feeling exactly like you're feeling. I just think if you reach out to help him, you'll help yourself."

"You sound like a therapist."

"It's just common sense."

"Thanks, Claire. Of course, you're right. I should start a letter to him."

"Exactly."

"And not worry so much about the long-term. Right?"

"Right. Just start the conversation with him and see where it goes. And enjoy the simple pleasure of knowing he'll answer your letters, and you'll answer his. There could be a future with him. It's still a possibility."

"I didn't expect this from you, Claire."

"What do you mean?" she said softly.

"Well, I knew you'd help me. But I imagined you'd brow-beat me into not wallowing and slap me around until I laughed at your stupid jokes again."

She smiled. "Yeah. Well. Whatever works." She paused. "So, how are you feeling about the frozen embryo?"

"Satisfied. Like I did my duty. I know the embryo will have a life. And, like you said, just being alive is pretty huge."

"So, you think you made the right decision?"

"Yeah. Absolutely. But I've been thinking a lot about how badly science has let women down. And how criminal it is women don't band together to demand a whole new approach, so unintended pregnancies can be pretty much eliminated. Like your idea—the one you called 'futuristic.' Why should it be futuristic? I refuse to believe it can't be done."

"I'm with you. Especially since it was my idea."

"Why in the world shouldn't we demand something better?"

"You're sounding like a woman who plans to do something about it."

"Yeah, Claire. I am."

"Good for you." I think she could see that I was exhausted. She stood and added, "Listen. I'll do the scar viewing tomorrow after school. It'll give me something to look forward to." She sighed. "I think you could use some rest."

"Yeah. Good idea."

She leaned over to give me a hug and I whispered, "Thanks so much, Claire. You've helped me a lot." She smiled at me and quietly left the room.

After she left, I drifted off and didn't wake until 4:00 a.m. I got up, walked stiffly over to my desk to sit, and opened my laptop. I paused to think for a couple of minutes, and then started typing.

My name is Eve Gehraghty and I'm sixteen years old. I am Patient X in Dr. Mary Hughey's recent article published in [name of medical journal to be inserted]. I'm writing this essay to explain my reasons for having the Retrieval and Preservation procedure.

The first time I really felt the intensity of the pro-choice vs. pro-life debate was when my family was planning a trip from our home in Chicago to the Women's March on Washington in January 2017. I had no way of knowing then that the argument my parents had about the march was a preview of the explosion that would happen— that I would cause—in 2020....

Author's Note

I've long been frustrated by the damage caused by the pressure from both sides of the abortion debate on their adherents to be single-issue voters. But it was the report that pro-life advocates wouldn't be welcome at the historic Women's March on Washington that started me thinking about writing this book. It struck me again that women won't be able to fully flex our political muscles until we come together on the things we do agree on—equal pay for equal work, harassment-free work environments, reasonable child-care, women's health issues, and a host of others.

It was around the time I started law school in 1975 that I began to self-identify as a feminist, and identifying as pro-choice seemed to be a logical part of the package. At the same time, I've never been able to completely ignore what abortion is—however we describe the embryo ("glob of cells" or "future baby").

Through pure luck, and probably my infertility issues, I'd never had to face what Eve does in the novel—an unwanted teen pregnancy. Those infertility issues were no longer my friend when my husband and I wanted to start a family. A little medical help allowed me to conceive our first daughter. But ten years and three IVF treatments later, she was still an only child. So, we adopted our second daughter. As any woman who's tried and failed to conceive knows, the whole process—from the highs of late periods to the lows of hopes dashed when the flow inevitably begins, from cherished pregnancy to devastating miscarriage—lands on the woman with a crushing weight.

But the flip-side—the weight of an unwanted pregnancy—has to be equally, if not more, crushing. With only anecdotal evidence to draw on, I needed to study the facts, the psychological impact, and the philosophical arguments about abortion. I pulled together and read everything I could get my hands on. What my analysis yielded surprised me.

In the novel, I've limited what Eve focuses on to what she sees as the "best arguments" on both sides. Obviously, there are many others. I don't presume to have the answer to anything. I've just tried to broaden the question a little. Please find discussion questions and other information at www.thetorontoembryo.com.

Acknowledgments

I suppose some writers can flesh out characters, straighten squidgy plot lines, massage dialogue and understand all of their research unassisted. If so, I'm not among them. I've always depended on the kindness of friends, especially when it comes to writing.

My only hesitancy in preparing my acknowledgments is my paranoia that I may leave someone out—probably a self-fulfilling prophecy. If it's you, please forgive me and know that I am deeply grateful for all of the input, advice, technical and medical information, and encouragement which have kept this project moving forward.

I'd like to begin by thanking the folks who provided me with invaluable scientific, medical, and other technical assistance, educating me in areas decidedly outside my realm of experience. Thanks to: Lorraine Fleck, Dr. Lynne Foreman, Russ Johnson, Max Langhorst BSN, RN, and Mary Beth Trybulec.

I'm also deeply grateful to those who explored the issues and the characters with me, acted as sounding-boards or beta readers, or offered the encouragement that kept me going. Thanks to: Betsy Ashton, Danielle Austin, Judith Budner, Amanda Cockrell, Shari Dragovich, Bridget Farmer, Holly Hale, Lily Helms, Sarah Hunter, Deborah Hurt-Saunders, Grace Kotre, Dr. John Kotre, the Lake Writers of Smith Mountain Lake, Pat Maloney, Mike Reed, Susan Reed, Deanna Stephens, Rev. Cheryl Wade, and Eileen Watson.

Special thanks to my publisher, Chuck Lumpkin of Snowy Day Publications, for his tireless and invaluable help in publishing this book, and to Tom Howell for using his considerable artistic talent to capture on the cover an image that existed only in my head.

Although I gave equal billing in my "bio" to our perennial puppies (after all, Chica the Brave did sit by me through every word of the book), their contribution rather pales in comparison with that of my husband. Larry got me back into creative writing after a 35-year hiatus, and working on short stories and novels makes me happy every day. He is mentor, muse, and motivator, and a writer with seriously scary talent. So, thank you so much, hon.

32686285R00128

Made in the USA
Columbia, SC
06 November 2018